Award-winning authors talk about *Simon Says*:

"Ms. Molly has, once again, woven her magical fiction in and out of the horrible reality of World War II, while we come under her spell and fall in love with her characters." —**Billie Letts, Author of *Where the Heart Is* and *The Honk and Holler Opening Soon***

"*Simon Says* is a moving story about eternal issues. Congratulations on a real accomplishment."—**Janice Shefelman, Author of *Comanche Song*, New York Public Library Best Books for the Teen Age**

Praise for Molly Griffis' other books:

The Rachel Resistance
Winner of the Oklahoma Book Award and Finalist for Tennessee's Volunteer State Book Award

"Griffis begins her story on 'a day that will live in infamy.' With humor and insight she richly documents America at the time of Pearl Harbor. Heroine Rachel Dalton is faced not only with a world that has to suddenly prepare for war, but also with the loss of her best friend, the departure of her beloved older brother for military service, and a continuing conflict with a suspicious and dangerous fellow student. Young readers will be moved and entertained. Older readers will sigh and say: 'Ah, yes, that is how it was!'" —**Earl Hamner, creator of *The Waltons***

The Feester Filibuster
Finalist for Tennessee's Volunteer State Book Award

"Griffis expertly captures this period of American history through the innocent eyes of a begrudgingly sensitive boy. Short chapters, colorful minor characters, and plenty of historical detail make this a fast and fulfilling read." —***Booklist***

"This is a compelling book, filled with humor, emotion, and well-drawn characters."—***School Library Journal***

"Molly Griffis can transport anyone back to the 1940s with ease. Her wonderful writing shows us the days when kids played with toys and not Game Boys. The days when war actually did affect everything. . . .

This well crafted tale will delight and fascinate children and even teenagers—even adults will find something to smile at. The book ends with a surprise ending that I won't spoil because unlike Rachel, I don't tell everything I know." —**Zephyr Goza, a young reader**

The Great American Bunion Derby
Finalist for the Oklahoma Book Award

"In a lively, down-home storytelling style, Griffis describes the 1927 International Trans-Continental Foot Race from the viewpoint of the winner, 20-year-old Andy Payne, a part-Cherokee farm boy from Oklahoma ... fun to read aloud. The design is spacious, and lively black-and-white photos are scattered throughout." —***Booklist***

"*The Great American Bunion Derby*—it's a grabber, it's a page turner. I was absolutely riveted. I ran every suspenseful and grueling mile with Andy Payne as he proved that a 'runner's heart' can overcome all obstacles. It left me with such a warm and fuzzy feeling, that I just didn't want it to end." —**Dennis Weaver, Actor**

"... a delightful addition for the runner's library. ...Ms. Griffis does a fine job of condensing the great race into a short, readable book, but to add to the delight, she includes a selection of photos that are priceless, including one of the customized Maxwell House Coffee truck that accompanied the runners to accommodate their caffeine needs." -**Rich Benyo, Editor, *Marathon and Beyond***

Buffalo in the Mall
Finalist for the Oklahoma Book Award

"A delightful book. A smile on every page." —**Anna Myers, Author**

"This rollicking book with whimsical illustrations ... is reminiscent of Ludwig Bemelman at his best." —**Gail E. Haley, Caldecott Medal Winner**

"A perfect book for children with its childlike wit. I found myself reading it over and over again to find the hidden jokes in the wonderful illustrations." —**Mike Wimmer, Illustrator and Finalist for the Texas Bluebonnet Award**

Simon Says

Molly Levite Griffis

EAKIN PRESS 🛡 Austin, Texas

FIRST EDITION
Copyright © 2004
By Molly Levite Griffis
Published in the U. S.A.
By Eakin Press
A Division of Sunbelt Media, Inc.
P.O. Drawer 90159
Austin, Texas 78709-0159
email: sales@eakinpress.com
website: www.eakinpress.com
ALL RIGHTS RESERVED.
1   2   3   4   5   6   7   8   9
1-57168-836-6 HB
1-57168-847-1 PB

Library of Congress Cataloging-in-Publication Data

Griffis, Molly Levite.
    Simon says / Molly Levite Griffis.– 1st ed.
        p.   cm.
    Summary: Simon, a sixth-grader who had been sent from Germany to
live with an American family when he was six years old, spends the
summer of 1942 facing his feelings of abandonment and learning about
anti-Semitism.
    ISBN 1-57168-836-6 (hb: alk. paper)
    1. World War, 1939-1945–Oklahoma–Juvenile fiction. [1. World War,
1939-1945–United States–Fiction. 2. World War, 1939-
1945–Jews–Rescue. 3. Jews–United States–Fiction. 4.
Antisemitism–Fiction. 5. Family–Fiction. 6. Identity–Fiction. 7.
Oklahoma–History–20th century–Fiction.] I. Title.
PZ7.G88165Si 2004
[Fic]–dc22   2004005465

J/Middle School

(Historical Fiction)

To those who say the Holocaust never happened, Simon says, "It did."

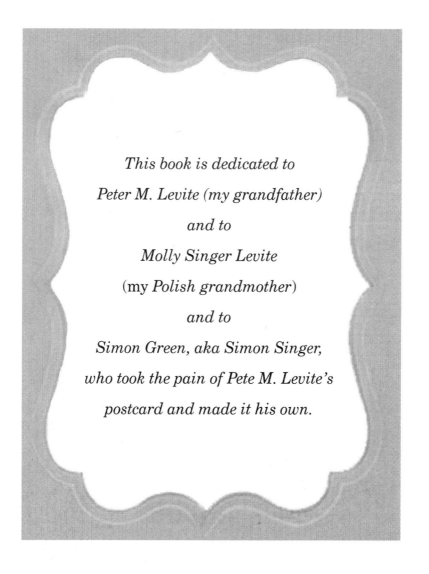

This book is dedicated to

Peter M. Levite (my grandfather)

and to

Molly Singer Levite

(my Polish grandmother)

and to

Simon Green, aka Simon Singer,

who took the pain of Pete M. Levite's

postcard and made it his own.

CONTENTS

CHAPTER 1
Postcard from the Past

August 3, 1942
Apache, Oklahoma

The postcard appeared in Simon Green's life for the first time the morning his best friend was moving away forever. Simon was frantically rummaging through an old trunk when he found it. The trunk was the only luggage still packed from the cross-country move he and his mother had made just before Pearl Harbor was bombed.

Simon had been looking for a baseball card for more than a week. That rare and wonderful George Herman "Babe" Ruth card was going to be the best present ever for the best friend ever, John Alan

Feester. The trunk in the basement was Simon's last hope.

"No need to even open this one!" his father had announced, slapping his hand on the trunk as the moving men loaded it onto the van in Pennsylvania. "Just a bunch of old books and manuscripts ... Store it and forget it!"

That was the reason Simon had put off looking in the trunk until last. That, and his fear of basements. Since the Babe Ruth card was the rarest of his collection, perhaps his father, who himself was moving into a navy barrack, had hidden the card in the old trunk and had forgotten to tell him.

The postcard was in a small tin box tucked in a back corner under layers of books, which included a leather-bound edition of John Alan's favorite, *Wind in the Willows*. For one moment, Simon considered using that book for his present. But since *Wind in the Willows* was written for little kids and John Alan was eleven years old now, he dismissed that idea and kept looking for the baseball card. He would never have given the postcard a second glance if the name on it had not exploded in his brain like the flashbulb on a camera of forgotten memories.

The postcard was addressed to the boy Simon Green used to be.

The boy named Simon Singer.

Simon Isadore Green, only son of Isadore and Sylvia Green, clutched the postcard with both fists and tried to keep his hands from shaking. Five years! It had been five years since he stopped being Simon Singer.

He stared at the postcard with its five postage stamps, all written in German. This postcard had been mailed to *him*. Why had he not received it? Why had someone hidden it in the bottom of this trunk?

"No need to even open this one!" his father had said. "Store it in the basement," he'd said. "Store it in the basement and forget it!"

His mother would not have hidden a postcard from him. They never kept secrets from each other, Simon Green and his mother. But his father, Isadore Green—who insisted Simon never talk about the past, never think about the past, never admit he *had* a past other than the one with them—yes, his father would have hidden Simon Singer's postcard.

But how important could a postcard be anyway? Simon wondered. *Postcards are too small for messages of any value. Only people on vacations send postcards!*

Simon studied the vaguely familiar Old World handwriting which had carefully scripted "Herr

Simon Singer" in the address box on the right front side. Underneath that long forgotten name was printed, in matching ink, "c/o Isadore Green"—along with the name and address of the company that published his father's books. The ink was black and had been smeared, evidently sometime after the card reached its final destination since parts of it were now quite illegible.

Simon's mouth turned dry as sawdust as he moved under the basement's only source of light, a bare bulb hanging by a cord from the ceiling. He was trying to decipher the Arabic numerals in the postmark:

Warsaw: 18 8 41

"August 18, 1941!" he called out as if he were a town crier who was paid to announce dates instead of hours. "A year ago this month!" he added in a whisper. "Before Pearl Harbor!"

Simon's heart moved outside his body as he turned the card over and continued to read aloud, even though there was no one to listen but himself.

"*Mein lieber Sohn* ... My dear son." He translated the German into English as smoothly as if he had been speaking German yesterday instead of five long years ago. But a salutation was easy, so easy

even an English-speaking American son could understand it with very little trouble.

The penman had switched to English for the
brief message.

"We are hungry.
Please to send us
something of bread."

Simon found himself whispering the writer's
plea for bread because the words were much too sor-
rowful to speak aloud.

The closing, too, was in English, except for one
word:

"Your lovely father and friend of the Jugend,
Bernard Singer."

It took Simon Green a while to remember that
Jugend meant "youth."

Simon stared at the postcard and then began to
turn it over and over in his hands as if he were a
magician performing a sleight of hand trick designed
to make it disappear.

But the postcard remained.

"We are hungry," he repeated. "*We* are ..."

We? His father and mother? His sister, Hannah? Even his Polish grandmother perhaps? Who were these hungry people, and why would they think he could send them bread? And didn't this Bernard Singer even know the difference between "lovely" and "loving"? What kind of love was that?

He held the card up closer to the bulb and examined every inch of it. There was no return address, no possible way Simon Singer could write to these people, no possible way he could send them "something of bread."

What were these hungry people doing in Warsaw anyway? Terrible things were being done to the Jews in Poland. He had read about it in the papers. Had they gone to look for his Polish grandmother? He had some memory of a journey to Poland, something his father had said perhaps. *His* father? Who was this man, Bernard Singer? Was it *his* father? But Isadore Green was his father! Why did Bernard Singer send a postcard to Simon Singer? What did Bernard Singer think Simon Singer could do?

Bernard Singer signed himself "friend of the youth." Simon thought about that. What kind of friend was he? A friend like John Alan Feester, who became his *best* friend and then moved away! Bernard Singer *sent* Simon Singer away, allowed him to be adopted by another family. Signed papers and put him on a boat to America.

None of this was his fault, Simon reasoned. This card had been sent a year ago. But if he'd read it the day it came, what could he have done? He looked at the postmark again: Warsaw, Poland. A city on the other side of the world, a city Simon Green knew nothing about.

That was why Isadore Green, his father, had not given him the postcard. Isadore Green, who was now serving in the United States Navy, loved his country and loved his son. He did not want to bother his son with a pitiful postcard asking for bread, a postcard his son could do nothing about.

Except for the day they arrived in Oklahoma, the day he had to help the moving man carry the trunk down the steep, icy cement steps, Simon had avoided the basement. The smell and the darkness picked at a corner of his brain like a fingernail worrying a crusty scab.

As he fingered the German stamps, Simon Green suddenly found himself staring at a giant swastika painted on the wall of a store, smelling the burning wood, hearing the glass shattering, tasting the acrid air. It was Simon Singer's *father's* store! And Simon Singer's *mother* worked in that store!

"Simon!" he heard a voice calling from upstairs. Sylvia Green's voice. *The* mother! He had not thought of her as *the* mother in many years. Sylvia Green was *his* mother. And she had all the bread she needed.

"Rachel's here!" Sylvia sang out in her perfect American English. "Come quickly! John Alan's father told me he wants an early start!"

John Alan . . . John Alan was moving today! Leaving him just like Bernard Singer left him on that ship to America. *Why should I give a present to a traitor like John Alan Feester, a traitor just like my father? For all I know, John Alan Feester might write me a postcard someday, too. He might even ask for something like my rare and wonderful Babe Ruth baseball card!*

Simon ran back to the trunk and was about to replace the postcard where he found it when he noticed two pieces of cloth in the bottom of the tin box. The first was a handkerchief. Since he'd forgotten his, he started to stuff it in his pants pocket when he noticed something embroidered on the corner. He held it up to the light and saw a red "S.S." His Polish grandmother had embroidered those initials there—Simon Singer's initials! He hesitated a moment, then stuffed the handkerchief down in his pocket as far as it would go.

The second cloth had been folded a number of

times to make a cushion for the postcard. He picked up one corner and watched as the doll-sized blue prayer shawl, fashioned from a table napkin, unfolded. He put the postcard down so he could rub the four knots his six-year-old fingers had tied. He had made this prayer shawl the first night he'd been in the Greens' home, made it for a doll, *his* doll, a doll he had to leave in Germany. A precious doll named ... named ... He could no longer remember the doll's name.

"Simon!" His mother's voice again, louder this time. "Rachel's waiting!"

He refolded the prayer shawl and slipped it in the hip pocket of his pants, but he put the postcard back in the tin box. He closed the lid and shoved the box back in the corner where he'd found it, willing himself to forget the postcard from Simon Singer's father. He was Simon Green, son of Isadore and Sylvia Green, and he had no memories of Simon Singer's family.

Except for his sister.

And his Polish grandmother.

And his mother.

And even his father.

"Simon," Rachel screamed down the stairwell, "if you don't come up here right now, I'm coming down there after you!"

She would, too. Rachel Elizabeth Dalton, whose initials spelled the color of her hair. Rachel was used to being obeyed. She would march down those stairs and haul Simon Green up the steps by his shirt collar. That was the kind of person she was. Sometimes Simon wondered why he and John Alan put up with her, why they liked her so much. But they did. Both of them.

As he stomped toward the stairs, he vowed to wipe his mind clean of the words on that postcard, erase them as if they were yesterday's homework chalked on a school blackboard. Simon Green was a born actor. Everybody said so. He could act as if he had never seen that postcard.

As for John Alan Feester's going-away present, John Alan didn't deserve a rare and wonderful baseball card for moving away any more than Bernard Singer deserved something of bread for giving his son away.

As his foot touched the first step, Simon began to count, first in German then in Polish, an exercise he had not performed since he was six years old. He had to concentrate very hard to recall that *eins* was one in German, *jeden* in Polish; two was *zwei* in German, *dwa* in Polish; *drei* was three in German, *trzy* in Polish. Perhaps having to remember German and

Polish numbers would be a good way to keep from having to remember German and Polish people.

But instead, every step Simon Green took out of that basement in Oklahoma in August of 1942 took him further and further into his past ... all the way back to 1937, when he first came to America.

CHAPTER 2
The Homecoming

June 13, 1937
Altoona, Pennsylvania

"Tell me, Simon, did you ever learn a little game that's played with just your thumbs?" Isadore Green asked at supper the first night six-year-old Simon Singer was in his new home. "It's a *following instructions* kind of game," the man added with an encouraging smile.

Simon, always the last in his family to finish any meal, picked up his napkin, wiped his mouth, and carefully smoothed the fringed blue cloth back on his lap again to give himself time to think.

Was this a trick question? He'd heard about

tricks being played on immigrant children, especially Jewish immigrant children, so he wasn't sure if he should answer truthfully or not. The truth was, he'd never heard of such a game until he was on the ship to America. Trude, the dark-haired girl from Maryland who became his friend, told him about it the first time she heard his name.

"Simon? Your name is really, truly Simon?" she had squealed, breaking into a sunny smile which reminded him of his sister, Hannah. He had to look away from that smile because thoughts of Hannah made his heart ache so much.

"Why, you're the boy my game was named for!" Trude went on when he looked back at her again. "My very favorite game! Do you know how to play the thumbs-up game?"

Simon shook his head back and forth, so she grabbed both of his hands, fashioned them into fists, and pulled his thumbs into upright positions.

"This game is called 'Simon Says,'" she whispered, as if she were passing on a military secret, "and here you are, my new friend, Simon! My mother says you are going to become an American. If that's true, you must learn how to play the American game named just for you!"

Simon had no idea where Trude's mother had

heard such a thing. He was going to America for a visit—a short visit of only a few months. Hannah had assured him of that. He was certainly not going to *become* an American. But he knew contradicting a mother was not polite, so he nodded his head, left his thumbs as Trude had positioned them, and learned to play her silly little game.

Simon examined the face of the man who now sat across from him at the square kitchen table with its crisp, white cloth and its crayon-colored dishes. The man's dark brown eyes, a mirror image of Simon's own, looked kind. Much kinder than the eyes of Simon's father, a man who could put his only son on a ship to America and make him promise not to wave good-bye. A man who *said* a wave might appear to be a *"Heil Hitler."* Simon didn't believe that for a minute. The truth was this: His father was in such a hurry to be rid of him, he wanted to leave the dock before a wave was necessary.

Who would think a Jewish boy, a boy who had seen and heard and smelled the Nazis for three whole years, would *ever* wish Adolph Hitler well? It was true Simon had once marched down the street in front of a parading Nazi band, pretending to be their director. Hannah had to rush into the street to drag him back— not an easy task since her lame leg made her movements slow and difficult. But he'd been a baby then, a three-year-old baby who liked parades. Now he was a six-year-old boy, a six-year-old boy who knew the truth about the Nazis and their terrible parades.

Simon sat both of his fists, thumbs up, on the table in front of him and nodded his head in a silent yes to the man's question about the game. His thick black hair, uncut for a long time, fell over his eyes, so he had to unclinch his fingers to push it back. He then dropped both hands into his lap and, without looking down, fingered the edge of his napkin until he came to a corner. He stopped and began to carefully tie a knot in the fringe.

The man named Isadore Green was still talking about the game.

"Well, when Max Burger, the man who brought you to us, the man who met your father and made the arrangements, when Max first told Sylvia and me about you, we decided immediately the game of Simon Says had been named especially for you." He smiled at the woman, who was heaping second helpings of roast beef as well as mashed potatoes and gravy onto Simon's plate, although he had not finished the first helpings yet. Her graceful hands floated over the dishes as if she were playing a piano, and her bright green eyes twinkled their approval of his every bite.

"You are obviously the kind of boy things *should* be named after!" Isadore Green enthused. "A boy who speaks three languages, reads in two of them, can add, subtract, multiply, and divide, but hasn't even started first grade! That's a truly remarkable boy! Such a boy should have a game, a building, perhaps even a library named for him! We feel very proud to have such a boy living in our home."

The man's lavish praise, laced with the fragrant smells of homemade bread and apple strudel, made Simon feel good all over, better than he had felt in a very long time. He read and understood English better than he spoke it, so he nodded his head in appreciation and murmured a simple "Thank you very much, sir and madam," rather than say more and perhaps shame himself. Hannah had warned him many times not to shame himself. He finished tying the final knot on the last corner of the napkin and resumed eating.

This napkin would make a nice prayer shawl for his Solomon doll, the doll Hannah was caring for while he was gone. The knots were not done as his Polish grandmother had taught him—the fringe was not long enough. But it would be better than no prayer shawl at all. Solomon's real prayer shawl had been lost the night the Gestapo burned their home and store and arrested his father. His mother had refused to let him go back to look for it, even though he begged her many times.

Simon wanted to bring Solomon with him to America, but his father said dolls were for babies, not six-year-old boys, and insisted his small cardboard suitcase only had room for practical things. Simon had explained he would rather do without his toothbrush, toothpowder, comb, and brush, but his father had other ideas. Unreasonable ideas. Like putting Simon on an ocean liner to America.

Sylvia Green refilled his milk glass and nodded her head in approval when he thanked her and patted his mouth with his napkin. This time he was careful not to raise it above the table edge because of the knots.

"What a polite, mannerly boy your mother has raised. She and your father must be very proud of you."

"My mother worked much in my father's store," Simon told her. "Hannah taught my manners to me."

"Yes," Sylvia replied. "We ... we read about Hannah in the letters Max wrote us. She must be very precious to you. Sisters always are."

Simon looked down at his plate and kept on eating, but he found swallowing much more difficult than it had been when he first began. He tried not to flinch when Isadore Green leaned all the way over the table to muss his hair with one hand and pat his shoulder with the other. Except for his Polish grandmother, Simon's family, even Hannah, did not often touch each other except to stay warm. The hugs these American strangers handed out so freely made him uneasy because he wasn't at all sure how to respond.

The three of them finished their meal in silence. The raucous cawing of two warring blue jays outside the kitchen window was the only sound in the room. The man and woman took turns smiling at each other and then at Simon, but neither said anything more until after the strudel had been served.

"It is quite a beautiful strudel, such loving icing," Simon said, speaking slowly and distinctly, hoping his violin-trained ear was allowing him to speak his English with no accent. His Polish grandmother assured him he spoke her language like a Pole. She said it was possible because of his musical training. He pretended his knife was a bow and took several small swipes over his strudel. He hadn't been allowed to bring his violin either.

"Do you want to telegraph to the world that you're a Jew?" his father had roared when he asked if he might bring it, and his mother and Hannah had begun to cry. In fact, in the two quick weeks between the day his father escaped from the concentration camp and the day Simon was sent away, his family had done little but shout and cry. As hard as it was to leave them, he had been almost relieved to get on a ship where there was no fighting, no Nazis, and more food than he had ever seen in his life.

Then he met Trude and learned to play her game. He colored with her crayons and listened to her stories about America. The Land of Opportunity, she called it. In no time at all, waking up became tolerable once more, even though he still looked for Hannah each time he opened his eyes.

When Simon finished scooping up every last flake of strudel with his knife and fork, he put them down on his plate, positioning them exactly as Isadore had positioned his. He wanted to ask the man why he had not used his knife to eat his meal, but he was unsure of the correct words to use.

He slid to the front of the wooden chair and clutched the sides of the seat with both hands to steady himself. Solomon's new prayer shawl was squeezed tightly between his knees.

Now that they had eaten, there were details to be discussed, important details about his future. Simon was sure of that. He was also sure it would be the adults who would do all the talking. That was the way it was in the world. Your father, your own flesh and blood, says he knows what's best for you. He doesn't once ask if it's okay with you. He tells you an American named Max is going to take you to America on a boat. And a few days later you are put on a boat in the company of this Max. Even Hannah said he had to go, although she admitted she had no idea who the man named Max was!

Isadore Green pushed his chair back from the table, reached for his pipe, and cleared his throat several times very loudly before he began to speak.

"You're a very smart boy, Simon, and so, while I'm sure you don't understand what has happened to you these past few weeks, you must know that in sending you to America, allowing Max to bring you to us, your father did ... Well, he did what he did because he thought it was the only way. The only way to save you from ..."

The man's voice grew softer and softer until Simon could no longer understand what he was saying. But that was all right because what the man was saying didn't make a lot of sense anyway. What did he mean "the only way"? How could he know that, this stranger? There were many ways, always many ways. It was just that his father did not choose to consider them. His father chose to send him away.

Simon switched his gaze from the man to the woman and back again and was relieved when it was the woman who began to talk this time.

"What Izzy is trying to tell you," she began slowly, "is that while he and I realize we could never replace your family, we would hope, for the time you are with us ... however long that might be ... you would consider us as two people who care about you a great deal and want to make you happy." She grabbed a strand of her short black hair between one finger and her thumb and began to twist it as if she were winding a long neglected clock.

"I am happy already," Simon assured her, nodding his head up and down vigorously. "You have a very nice house and a very nice food. It was such a beautiful strudel. I am very, very happy here already. I am—" He stopped because he was afraid he was beginning to sound a little scared, even a little desperate, perhaps. These strangers were his last hope. If they decided to send him away like his father did— in a strange country where he knew no one, without Hannah to help him—well, he just had to stay with these people until it was time for him to go home.

Simon studied Sylvia Green, a slender, pretty, healthy-looking woman, much healthier-looking than the mother he had left behind. Sylvia gave him a warm smile and crooked her finger at him invitingly. Clutching the napkin prayer shawl in one hand, he went over and stood beside her chair. She patted him on the back before she gently lifted him onto her lap. He had not sat on a lap since the night his Polish grandmother had been taken by the Nazis. Hannah's lame leg prevented her from holding him that way. Sylvia stroked his hair and hummed a little tune in his ear, a German folk song he instantly recognized. He began to hum along, fingering the strings of an imaginary violin.

"Your sad, sad homeland, Simon," she whispered in his ear when her song ended, "it was my dear parents' homeland, too." She sighed as she added, "I think we've talked enough for one night, Simon Says. It's been a very long day for you. I'll wash the dishes while Isadore gets you to bed. We'll talk again in the morning, when the world's been born again, and we've all had sweet dreams. Okay?" she questioned as she took his face in her hands and planted a soft kiss on his forehead.

"Okay!" Simon echoed as he slid off her lap, transferred his prayer cloth napkin to his right hand, and took Isadore Green's hand with his left.

"Okay is my favorite word of all time," Simon confided to Isadore as they trudged up the stairs to his new bedroom. "It is in German the same as in English. I like the way my mouth feels to say it, and I like that the person who asks it wants to know what I think!" He was silent for several steps before he added, without looking up, "My father never once asked for my okay. He just sent me away."

Isadore paused for a moment and threw his head back to stare at the ceiling above the stairs. Then he squeezed Simon's hand gently as he slowed his big steps to match the boy's smaller ones.

"Sylvie and I hope to make everything okay for you again, Simon. Everything we possibly can."

He had often wished to live in a two-story house, Simon reminded himself as he continued climbing the stairs, counting the steps in his head, first in German, then in Polish so he wouldn't forget. He always counted steps, always wanted to know exactly how far up or down it was to any destination. There were twenty-two steps down to the dirt floor of the basement of the house where he lived last, and only four to the kitchen of the home and store that were no more.

CHAPTER 3
A Room of His Own

"You're a big boy, Simon, and after all you've been through, I imagine you'd enjoy some privacy," the man said as he opened the door to the bedroom to the right of the stairway. "I'll let you put on your pajamas and get yourself into bed." He started to leave but turned around again to add "Okay?" before he winked and ruffled Simon's hair one final time. He waited for Simon's emphatic "Okay!" before he left, closing the door behind him.

Simon sighed and looked around his room for the second time. Sylvia had led him straight upstairs when they first arrived and helped him empty his suitcase into the chest of drawers.

"This is your room to do with as you choose," she

had told him as she threw open the door with a flourish. "It's small and a bit plain because Izzy and I couldn't agree on what pictures you might like. The best thing about a log house . . . Izzy and I built this one together . . . is you can thumbtack any picture you want any place at all and then take it down the next day if you change your mind! I have stacks of magazines you can go through and cut out all kinds of things. Birds, airplanes, automobiles . . . whatever you like to look at."

Simon had been so surprised to have an entire room all to himself, he could only smile and nod, but now he carefully studied the bedroom from floor to ceiling. The wood floor was polished to a high glow and contrasted sharply with the rough surface of the wall logs. The brown chest, which had four drawers, sat next to the bed. A nightstand with a lamp on it was the only other furniture, but a large globe of the world and another small one of the planet Mars, each on waist-high wooden stands, filled the room nicely.

Simon rotated the larger ball, tracing his fingers over the bumpy surface until he located Germany, which was black. When he found it, he tried to measure the distance to America, which was gold, with his thumb and little finger. The span was only a matter of inches, but his hand was too small to bridge the gap. He put both hands together, thumb to thumb, and smiled when he was able to make the tips of each little finger touch the borders of the two countries. He studied his thumbs a moment and then made fists pointing them toward the ceiling.

"Simon says, 'Go home!'" he whispered softly before he turned from the globe and walked to the window to watch the moon rise over the treetops.

It was some time before Simon stripped off his clothes, dropped them on the floor, and put on the new red-and-white-striped pajamas Sylvia had placed on the chest for him. As he climbed into bed, the first real bed in a long time, he tried very hard not to think of Hannah huddled on their straw-filled pallet on the basement floor. Their mother had the only bed in the sparsely furnished place. Even in the summer, the dirt below their pallet was always cold and damp, and Hannah had trouble getting up and down from it. Simon tried not to see her waiting for him, but her face and outstretched arms filled his head.

He picked up the blue napkin and rubbed it between his fingers and thumbs. He held it by either corner and pulled the smooth edge back and forth under his nose. He'd done that with his blanket when he was a baby, Hannah told him, rubbed the edges back and forth until the satin binding was worn away entirely. He always went to sleep doing that, she said.

He kissed his fingertips and blew a kiss in the direction he thought Germany to be. Although she rarely hugged him, Hannah often blew him kisses, and when he closed his eyes, he could picture her fingers on her pale pink lips.

He was about to drift off to sleep when he remembered something very important. He sat up in bed, carefully smoothed his prayer shawl on the pillow, and sprang to the floor. In the darkness, he made his way to the chest and rummaged through the bottom drawer, the one which held the contents of his suitcase. The top three were full when he arrived, stuffed with new toys, new clothes, towels, and bedding. But the bottom drawer, the easiest for him to reach, held the only possessions he knew for sure belonged to him.

He crept back to the bed, pulled off the pillow, and placed it on the floor in front of the chest. Then he carefully slid the heavy drawer out of its slot and onto the pillow so he could quietly drag it over to the window where a small section of the floor was bathed in moonlight. Living in a basement had made him part mole, his mother often told him. His mother. She would have thought this room quite a waste of space for just one person.

He ran his fingers over the brown jacket Hannah had once worn. It had been altered to fit him, but not very carefully. His mother and needles were not good friends, or so his Polish grandmother said. He held the jacket close to his face, hoping that the scent of Hannah remained in its folds. She was still there! He took a deep breath and held it for as long as he could.

A pair of pants, cut from his mother's green wool skirt, lay under the jacket, but no matter how hard he sniffed, he could not smell his mother. Three very worn, much too small shirts held no memories at all, and the two pairs of underwear were so tattered he felt ashamed when he looked at them.

On the bottom of the stack were the bright red stocking cap and gloves his Polish grandmother had knitted for him. He hugged them to his chest before he reached into the cap and slipped out a little book and pencil, which had been carefully wrapped up together in a cream-colored handkerchief.

Simon Singer unfolded the handkerchief, trying not to look at the initials embroidered on one corner in dark red thread. His Polish grandmother had put them there long ago: S.S. Although they were small, smaller than his smallest fingernail, he wished they were not there, wished those were not his initials. He folded the handkerchief where he could not see his grandmother's handiwork and opened his daybook to the last entry.

"June 12, 1937," he read aloud to the moon. "Age six years, 25 days."

Simon kept track of his exact age, wrote it in his daybook every night. When a person died, the stone-cutter needed to know his exact age in order to chisel it on the tombstone, and Simon wanted to be sure the date on his tombstone was correct. Under his age he had written: "New York. Max. Train. Isadore and Sylvia Green."

He turned the page, licked his pencil, and began writing: "June 13, 1937. Age six years, 26 days. Pennsylvania. My room." He glanced toward the globe before he added, "Germany is black and far away."

CHAPTER 4
A New Day

A bird awakened him the next morning, a bird singing such a happy song Simon was sure it had just uncovered a nest of worms. That is, if American worms lived in nests. He'd have to remember to ask Isadore about that. Isadore seemed to know a lot about birds. In the car, when Simon admitted to a great interest in birds, Isadore began to enthusiastically name each species flitting past the windows. He discussed their habits in detail as the car, driven by Sylvia, bumped its way along the dusty road toward home.

Home. *Heimat. Dom.* Simon rolled the word over his tongue in three languages as he looked around the sun-drenched room. He had not had a home since the Nazis, with their horrible red, black, and white swastika and their terrible black boots, stomped into his life. A soft knock pulled him from that image to the door.

"Well, happy fourteenth of June, Simon," Isadore cried. "It's Flag Day in Pennsylvania!" He clicked his heels together and snapped his hand to his forehead in a military salute.

Simon paused for a moment before he smiled and saluted back, trying to hold his hand exactly as the man held his.

"Since you're going to live in Pennsylvania, you need to know all the state holidays. We've been celebrating Flag Day since 1893. You're dressed for the occasion in those red-and-white-striped pajamas! American flag colors! All you need is a blue and white field of stars on your chest, and you could lead the parade!"

Simon started to say he didn't care for parades but changed his mind. Instead, he solemnly walked his fingers over the bars on his chest and asked, "How many stripes on the flag of America?"

"Seven red, six white, and a star for each of the forty-eight states. But we'll save the rest of our history lesson until after breakfast. I'm starved, and as every English speaker needs to know, the early bird gets the worm! That's an 'old saw' I just said. You'll be learning lots of those."

"Saw? Like what is used to cut a tree?"

"Nope, old saws aren't sharp. In fact, most of them have been used so often they're pretty dull. But a person learning English needs to know them. Old saws are wise sayings that have been around a long time. If you want some of Sylvie's tasty breakfast worms, you'd better run downstairs fast! If I get there first, there won't be a single worm left! I'll be the early bird, understand?"

"But what if a person does not *like* to eat worms?" Simon giggled as he shoved his feet into new red house shoes. "What does he do then, Mr. Izzy, this worm-disliking person?" He bent over, touched his toes, and yelled, "I would race you to the table!" before he charged down the stairs two at a time. He glanced back over his shoulder at the man who was laughing and shaking his head as if something had surprised him greatly. The man then charged after him, pushing and shoving as if he, too, were a hungry six-year-old.

Simon's father had never raced him, not even when Simon teased and begged him to do so. Bernard Singer spent all his time worrying about running away from the Nazis and never once ran away from

Simon just for fun. He could have done that at least once, but he never did.

As he watched Isadore Green collapse into his kitchen chair, laughing and holding his side as if he had a stitch, Simon wished his father could see what fun it was to race. To laugh. Well, it was his own fault. He could have come with Simon if he had really wanted to. He could be running around this kitchen right now! His father, his mother, and Hannah, too, although Hannah could not run. His father had been smart enough to escape that prison, so why had he not been smart enough to bring them all to America?

"Well, Sylvie, my love, looks like we've got ourselves another Glenn Cunningham here! Not only is this boy smart, but he can also run."

"Who is this Cunningham who can run?" Simon wanted to know as he grabbed his napkin, threw it into his lap, and picked up a biscuit in each hand. "He is faster than me? Are you sure? How can you be sure if this Cunningham and I have never raced? I am very, very hungry. I sleep very, very nice. I am very, very glad to be here! Is there butter for this nice bread?"

"Hold your horses, partner!" Isadore Green told him, gently prying one of the biscuits out of his hand and putting it back down on his plate. "Here's the butter, but use the butter knife this time. It's that small one next to the plate."

"And this knife," Simon asked, picking up the one that was next to his spoon, "why do you not eat your food with this one? It is much handy that way."

"Much handi*er*," Isadore corrected. "And I'm not sure why we do it the way we do in America, but that knife is used only for cutting, not for a scoop to get food on your fork. Such a lot to learn. But you won't have any trouble. Just watch and ask questions. I'm about to decide question asking won't be as much of a problem for you as I thought."

"I told you the cat had his tongue last night," Sylvia laughed as she spooned fried potatoes and scrambled eggs onto all three plates.

"A cat? You own a cat? Where is this cat?" Simon cried, squinting at the screen door which led to the back porch.

"Nope, sorry to say we are fresh out of cats right now, Simon. Dogs, too. But I imagine your arrival will change that." Isadore smiled as he put the butter knife back on the butter plate under Simon's watchful eye. "Sylvie just used another of those old saws I told you about. English is full of them. Saying the cat's got a person's tongue," he stuck his own tongue out and pinched it between his fingers, "just means the person is being very quiet." He paused before he added, "Probably because he is worried or scared."

Simon stopped eating and looked down at his plate. He bit down on his tongue to be sure it was still where it was supposed to be.

"After you went to bed," Sylvia hurried on, "I told Izzy I didn't think you were really the very quiet boy you pretended to be last night. I said I was sure you were putting on an act for us. Our friend Max says you love to act, that you told him you planned to be an actor someday ... as well as a zookeeper, a concert violinist, a doctor, and a postman!" She mussed his hair again. This time it felt quite good. "You have been through some very bad times, my little Simon Says, very hard times, but Isadore and I plan to make up for them."

Simon's mouth was so full of biscuit he was only able to nod his head. This hugging and patting might not be so bad. It would just take some getting used to. This woman was a very good cook. His mother had not been such a cook. Of course, there had been very little food for her to prepare, but what she did fix never tasted very good. Still, Esther Singer loved him. Loved him very much. He knew that. And yet, if he remembered the bad times ... the times she slapped him for yelling bad words at the Nazis ... the times she pinched him for eating Hannah's piece of bread even though Hannah told him to ... the time she caught him throwing paint on a swastika. If he remembered those times, it made it easier not to miss her. He reached for his second biscuit. As he broke it, he saw Hannah's hungry eyes watching him.

"This Cunningham person, the runner," Simon said, to remove Hannah's eyes from his mind, "tell me about him. Is he American? Finland has many good runners. My father spoke of them. My father was a runner as a boy. He said it was good training for running away from the Nazis." He took another bite before he added, "I am not really a very good runner. The Nazis could catch me very easy."

Isadore and Sylvia both put their forks down and looked at him, making Simon wonder if perhaps "Nazis" was not a proper word to use at the table. His mother often corrected him for saying certain words at the table. She insisted there were words that disturbed digestion. Those words should not be spoken at a meal, even when they no longer had a table to eat from.

"Well, Cunningham's a pretty amazing fellow," Isadore finally replied. "I did a *Time* magazine story about him once. That's the name of a magazine I write for when I'm not writing books. *Time*, it's called. Got to know him pretty well. Even went over to Kansas for an interview. He was burned in a fire when he was your age. They didn't think he'd ever walk again, much less run. Takes him an hour of rubbing every race to get those scarred legs of his ready. But he set a world record in the mile, and last year he won a silver medal in the Berlin Olympics!"

At the mention of Berlin and the Olympic games, Simon stopped eating and looked from Sylvia to Isadore and back again, but both of them were looking down at their plates. Could they discuss Hitler and those Olympic games at the table? Surely they heard the terrible things Hitler said about the black American runner who won four gold medals and shamed the Germans. Even Simon heard *that* story. He waited, but they said nothing about Hitler.

Simon finally broke the silence. "I would like to read about this man Cunningham," he said, "if you have your magazine still. Because of Effie, I read my English better than I talk my English."

"And who was Effie, my sweet?" Sylvia asked, sounding eager to change the subject once more.

"Effie was the American wife of my father's friend, Hans," Simon replied between bites. "Effie was once a famous actress! Then she stopped being a famous actress to become Hans' wife. She taught

Hannah and me English speaking and reading and acting. We stayed in their basement, my mother, Hannah, and me, while my father was in the concentration camp. We were there a long time. Effie took us upstairs for our school and our plays. We studied every day, and I could practice my violin there. I had a desk, but Hannah had to sit at the table. Because of her leg. We even had a stage in one room. It had a real curtain made of a red velvet bedspread!"

"Hannah ... was ... was crippled, wasn't she?" Sylvia asked, speaking as if she were talking more to herself than to him, so Simon simply nodded.

"Effie had many books," he went on, "and American relatives sent her packaged food. She had a friend at the post office. He got them through for her. She would bring the books and food down to us. Often the food was still in boxes. I started learning English by reading those boxes. 'Open this end!' 'Shake well before opening!' 'Cook before ingesting!' Effie used the boxes for my teaching, too!" He grinned as he added, "That's why I play very good Simon Says. I can follow directions!" He took the last bite of his potatoes. "My reading is better than my speaking. In the basement, it was safer to read than to talk. The Nazis could not hear us read."

Sylvia jumped up and started to give him more

scrambled eggs, but Simon covered the plate with his hands and shook his head, so she reluctantly sat down again.

"Speaking of reading, we got you a present, Simon," Isadore said, jerking Simon's thoughts from the basement to the kitchen table once more. "Since you had to celebrate your birthday on the boat, Max said you didn't get any presents. So, we'll celebrate your birthday today! When you finish your breakfast, we'll show you what we got for you."

Simon was almost too excited to eat, but he was so hungry he couldn't stop. So he couldn't talk either. Hannah had been very strict about him talking with his mouth full. Even when they were living in a basement, she made him use his napkin and chew with his mouth closed.

When he finished his breakfast, Sylvia walked over and scooted his chair out from the table for him as she said, "Now we'll go see your birthday present. Close your eyes and count to ten ... in German if you want."

"No!" Isadore commanded, slapping his hand on the table so hard the silver clattered on the plates. "No German! Not a word of German is ever to be spoken in this house again!"

Simon busied himself with rearranging his knife

and fork in the correct positions so he wouldn't have to look at either of them.

"Oh, Izzy, no! He's lost his family, his country! Don't take away his language, too! Not this soon," Sylvia pleaded before Isadore's eyes silenced her. Simon had seen his mother silenced by his father in the same way. Many times.

"The birthday present will have to wait," Isadore said, grabbing Simon by the shoulders and leading him out of the kitchen and over to an enormous chair in the corner of the small living room. "Sit down," he commanded again, and Simon climbed into the soft, overstuffed chair. His feet dangled several inches above the floor and made him feel very small.

"There's another old saw you need to learn today, Simon," Isadore said in a voice suddenly so ice-pick sharp it chipped his words in the air. "Actually, it's a proverb. A famous American named Benjamin Franklin said it. It goes like this: 'Three may keep a secret, if two of them are dead.'"

Simon's eyes grew very big as he contemplated the famous American's words. He mentally translated them first into German and then into Polish. The proverb delivered the same threatening message in all three languages.

Simon looked from Isadore to Sylvia and back

again. There were three of them in this room right now. Did Isadore Green mean that two of them were going to have to die because of some secret which was about to be revealed? Death had often come quickly and surprisingly back in Germany. Perhaps it did in America, too. Perhaps these people were not as kind and good as they seemed to be!

Simon sat up straight and clutched the arms of the chair with both hands. He pulled his legs straight up in the air, as if he were trying to keep some unseen crocodile from biting off his feet, and waited for Isadore Green to reveal the secret.

CHAPTER 5
A New Life

"Izzy! You're scaring the child out of his wits!" Sylvia cried when she saw Simon's reaction to her husband's words. "This boy's heard far too much about death and dying already ... I'm not going to let you ..."

"Simon," Isadore said, going over to push the boy's legs back down so he could kneel in front of him, "I'm ... I'm sorry. I didn't mean to frighten you, but you must understand the seriousness of our situation here. It's a sad fact of life that the world is a very scary place right now, and it is getting worse every minute! Each day we learn about some new terrible thing being done to the Jews in Germany. In other parts of Europe, too. The horror is spreading like fire in a dry forest soaked with gasoline. Swastikas have even appeared on American walls ... in American cities. Windows here have been broken."

He paused to give another silencing look to Sylvia, who was moaning softly and shifting her eyes from the man to the child and back again as if she were watching a fast-paced tennis match.

"Hatred of Jews is not new. You know that, Simon. That's why, when my father came to this country with the name Greenberg on his passport, he, like a lot of other people, decided to forsake his name—forsake, but not forget. And he became Carl with a 'C' *Green* instead of Karl with a 'K' *Greenberg*. I was a child, your age, in fact, and I refused to change my first name even though he told me Isadore was a Yiddish name ... a Jewish name. I had been Isadore for six years, and I wouldn't, *couldn't* give it up. But I did ... I have ... repeatedly denied my Jewish heritage ... said that I had no religion ... refused to admit it, even on my book jackets. That's the *main* reason your father agreed to let us ..."

Isadore Green was staring out the window now, staring as if he were looking for something or someone he had lost, something or someone that had run away from him. It was several minutes before he turned back to Simon, long minutes in which the only sound in the room was the ticking of the grand-father clock.

"I have decided it is absolutely necessary no one knows you came to us from Germany, that no one knows you have family back there. It will be better if all three of us forget your past entirely. Wipe it clean as that strudel plate of yours last night."

Simon opened his mouth to object, but thought better of it. He needed to hear everything this man had to say, needed to wait and see if this man was going to ask for his opinion, ask for his okay. His father had not. This man might not either.

"Only if we are directly asked will we admit you are adopted, because that is what we are going to do, Simon, we are going to adopt you. We are going to be your father and mother."

Simon's eyes grew wider. He had a mother already. And a father, too, although his father had . . . What was it his father had done?

"Pretending you were our child by birth might cause problems down the line, blood types that don't match, things like that. But for your own protection, for your safety, we shall say we adopted you from an orphanage here in America, adopted a tiny American baby boy. That way, if something should happen—if somehow the Nazis take over all of Europe and then come here looking for Jews ... Well, all I can say is it would be better if your life, your history, began with us ... here ... in this room ... today."

Simon looked from the man to the woman. She was staring at the floor and clutching her hands together so tightly her knuckles were turning white.

"Max got us the necessary paperwork, handled all the legalities of your adoption. Your father signed the papers. Max is a very smart fellow, a very ... influential person." Isadore chewed his lip as he added, "We who could acquire such papers and get a child such as you ... *we* are the lucky ones. So many are left over there, so many who will never. .. "

Simon sat and puzzled over what the man had just said. His father had signed the papers? What did that mean? What kind of papers were there that said your son was no longer your son, that your father was no longer your father?

The room was silent again, except for the clock. Simon shifted his eyes to the enormous face. He could tell time, had taught himself when he learned to multiply. At one time he even owned his own pocket watch. His Polish grandmother brought it when she came to live with them, but it, too, had been lost when the Nazis came to take her. The watch had belonged to his grandfather, the grandfather he would never know.

45

The Nazis had come for his Polish grandmother before they came for his German father. And now Isadore Green was telling him the Nazis might even come to America looking for him. All the way across the ocean! The S.S., Hitler's *Schultastaffel,* with their horrible swastika, might come looking for him in Pennsylvania of America! He had never thought of such a thing.

Simon squinted at the clock's face. The minutes and hours were painted in gold Roman numerals, which were harder for him to read. He had to take his finger and point and count to be sure he was telling the time correctly. While his family was in the basement, he had decided that clocks and watches were of little value since they only marked off the minutes and hours of one day. Clocks knew nothing of the future, and if you forgot to wind them, they told you nothing at all.

"You are our family's future, Simon," his mother had whispered when she hugged him good-bye. Her words had surprised him as much as her hug.

How could he be his family's future if he forgot his past? Perhaps he could ask Isadore for more papers, papers for his family, at least for Hannah. What would such papers say? In what language would they be written? Where would such papers be sent? He had overheard his father telling his mother they would be leaving the basement soon, going to Poland to search for his grandmother. But what about Hannah? It was very hard for Hannah to travel. There was no way to . . .

He looked back at Isadore Green. This man had kind eyes, eyes that looked as if he wanted something very badly. They were the eyes of a man who would never send his son away.

Isadore smiled at him and mouthed the single word, "Okay?"

Simon returned the smile and turned to look at Sylvia again. She was still staring at her hands, soft hands that felt so good when she patted his cheek. She would never yell at him for throwing paint on a swastika. Life would be nice here in this house.

But to give up Hannah, to give up Germany! There had to be other ways. There were always other ways.

Suddenly, it all became very simple.

He could *act* the part of this American boy Isadore Green wanted him to be, act the part of an American boy the Nazis knew nothing about. He was very good at charades, very good at reciting monologues. Effie told him that many times, and Effie had been a famous actress! She had directed many plays for Hannah and him, plays where he could run and jump and Hannah was not required to move at all. They did the Billy Goats Gruff, and he played all the goats wearing a costume made from a burlap potato bag, while Hannah played the troll under the bridge. He was a very good actor!

So he would act the part of this boy, this son of Isadore and Sylvia Green, and then someday, when the opportunity came—America was the Land of Opportunity—he would return to Germany and become Simon Singer, son of Bernard and Esther Singer once more.

These were kind people, good people. They would not mind if he were their son for just a little while. But, just in case Isadore might not think his idea was a good one, he would wait to tell him of his plan until he was leaving Pennsylvania to go home again.

"O-*kay*," Simon said slowly, breaking the word into two long syllables that pulled his lips into a smile. "What is the name of this new boy I am supposed to be and what things has he done?"

CHAPTER 6
Simon Isadore Green

"Well, o-*kay!*" Isadore shouted back, releasing his breath in one great rush and slapping his hands together at the same time. "First of all, you are still Simon. I wouldn't give up my first name, and I would not ask you to give up yours. But since our name is Green, and you are now our son, your name will be Simon Isadore Green."

"But Izzy, I thought ... you told me ..." Sylvia interrupted, tears falling from her words, "you said we were just taking him in for a little while to save him ... that his parents would ..."

"We'll discuss this later, Sylvie! I know the best plan for the three of us, you and Simon and me. For my family. Max and I have worked out all of the

49

details. Every last detail. I am a writer, and I can write fiction as well as fact! I create lives for people, and I have created a new life for Simon. The day Max called me about this boy, I began to write the biography of Simon Green."

"*My* biography?" Simon cried, jumping out of the chair and running over to position himself between Isadore's knees. "I know about biographies! The word is the same in German as in English. I have even read a biography, the biography of Wilhelm Richard Wagner! Effie got it for me! I thought only famous people who lived a very long time had biographies written about them!"

"Well, I said you're the kind of person things *should* be named after, biographies *should* be written about. And so I wrote yours! I'll read it to you for now, so I can answer any questions you might have, but I'm sure that before too long, you'll be able to read it to yourself. It's rather short, but then you are a rather short person," he laughed as he handed Simon a sheaf of papers bound with leather front and back and laced together with a thin gold string. On the front cover, lettered in gold much like the lettering on the clock, was the title *The Tale of Simon Green*.

"*The Tale of Simon Green*! Just like *The Tale of Peter Rabbit*!" Simon cried, hugging the book to his chest. "*Peter Rabbit* is my best book! I had it with me on the ship!" He dropped his chin to his chest and in a whisper added, "But I left it behind ..."

"We'll get you another copy!" Sylvia assured him. "The next time we go to town. *The Tale of Peter Rabbit* will be the very first book we buy."

Simon looked back up at her and smiled. "Effie said I hopped around her house like Peter. She even called me Peter sometimes. Peter Rabbit ran fast! That is why he was able to escape the Nazi farmer!" Once again the looks on their faces told him he had said something wrong, but since he didn't know what it was, he went on. "My Polish grandfather's name was Peter, and my Polish grandmother gave me the Peter Rabbit book. My Polish grandfather was—" He stopped in midsentence. "Did I ... do I ... does Simon Isadore Green have a Polish grandmother? Did he have a Polish grandfather who left him his watch?"

"Izzy, I *really* don't think this is going. .." Sylvia tried to interject, but his eyes sliced her words into little pieces.

"Unfortunately, Simon, the only grandparents you could have any knowledge of would be our parents, Sylvie's and mine, and neither of our fathers was from Poland. All our people were from Germany. And sadly, our parents are dead. That fact, and the fact that we are so isolated, so far from other people, that's what made my idea about adopting you workable.

"We are loners, Sylvie and I, as well as very private people. We've been living way out here for seven years now, since I sold my first novel. The few friends we do have would not be surprised to find we had adopted a child and neglected to tell them about it. We're great secret keepers, and since you are our son, I'm sure you can be, too. But, in answer to your questions, I'm sorry to say that Simon Green had no Polish grandparents."

Simon clamped his jaws shut and stuck his lower lip out, a habit that made his father very angry. But, since his father wasn't here, and he had no idea how Isadore Green felt about lips, he stuck it out as far as it would go and left it there while he walked over to the couch, sat down, and prepared to listen to the reading of *The Tale of Simon Green*.

"Simon Isadore Green was a foundling," Isadore began, pronouncing the new word carefully, "which means a baby left on the steps of an orphanage. Therefore, this lucky boy gets to celebrate two birthdays each year!"

"Two birthdays!" Simon crowed. "What a nice

way for this new boy to start his new life! I am liking being this new boy already!"

In the next paragraph, the orphanage doctor was quoted as saying he chose May 17, 1931 (Simon Singer's real birthdate) to go on the official birth certificate because of the stage of healing of the baby's belly button the day he was found. Simon didn't have to ask what a belly button was, since he had examined his own for quite some time after an older boy on the ship answered all his questions about birth and sex—questions his parents wouldn't answer.

Since his father had repeatedly told people Simon looked like a rat the first months of his life, he loved his biographer saying he was such a beautiful baby, such an appealing baby, that his stay in the orphanage was a very short one. On August 26, 1931, the second birthday he would get to observe, he was happily and joyfully adopted by Isadore and Sylvia Green of rural Altoona, Pennsylvania, who had always wanted a son of their own. He had no aunts, no uncles, no cousins, no grandparents—just a father and a mother.

Many of the details of Simon Singer's life—the fact he had taught himself to read, that he could do math problems by the age of six—were enlarged and embellished with details to make his early life as

Simon Green both American and Pennsylvanian. He taught himself to read from the backs of cereal boxes while riding in a grocery cart at the A & P in Altoona. His mother, Sylvia Green, virtuoso, had taught him to play the violin. A virtuoso, it was explained, was a very good violinist.

"You play the violin?" Simon shouted at Sylvia when Isadore reached that fact in his biography. "You really truly play a violin?"

"I do play the violin, sweet Simon. Just like you! We ordered you a half size the minute we found out you could not bring yours with you. We had hoped it would be here by now, but it's not. And that fancy word 'virtuoso' is just your biographer's way of saying I'm a pretty fair fiddle player."

"What is the word 'fiddle'?" Simon wanted to know.

"Just another word for violin. Sylvie likes to call herself a fiddler since fiddle players are usually country folks whose fiddles are made from cigar boxes!"

"I am not a very good fiddle player anymore," Simon sighed. "I am not able to practice like I should. But I shall try not to squeak loud."

"Loudly. Squeak *loudly*," Sylvia corrected. "That's the best thing about living out here. There's nobody to complain but the blue jays! Your skill will come back quickly. Playing the violin is like riding a bicycle

... once you learn how, you never really forget! By fall, we'll be playing duets, you and I."

Simon gave a happy shrug and signaled for Isadore to begin reading again. When he learned that Simon Green was particularly fond of Groundhog Day, he questioned, "Who is this hog of the ground I enjoy to go see ... the one who searches for his shadow? Can we really go to help him find it?"

"Groundhog, not hog of the ground," Isadore laughed, "and yes, indeed, we'll be going to see him next spring and every spring thereafter! He's a furry little animal that comes out once a year to predict the weather. That groundhog up in Punxsutawney is Pennsylvania's pride."

"Oh, sweet Simon Says!" Sylvia sighed. "There's so much we want to teach you, so much we want to do for you!"

When Isadore got to the last page of Simon's biography, he motioned for him to get up from the couch.

"Max says you enjoy acting—says you're quite good, in fact. Says you won the ship's talent show with a Charlie Chaplin monologue that had the audience laughing long and loud. He also said your Effie actually had you and Hannah doing Shakespeare! Why don't you act out this last page of your life? We'd love to see you on stage!"

"Okay, sir and madam," Simon intoned dramatically as he wiggled off the couch to take his biography in his hand and stand in front of them. What better way to start his new life? He had decided he could act the part of Simon Green, and here he was—acting! Consulting his biography as if it were a play script, he paced back and forth as Effie had taught him to do when he was playing Hamlet.

"Simon Green, a very real boy," he let go of his script with one hand and pointed to himself, "will live happily ever after with his very real parents, Isadore and Sylvia Green!" He paused to point again as he named them, trying to guess how his biographer was going to end this *Tale of Simon Green.*

"How did Simon Green know Isadore and Sylvia Green were his *real* parents?" Simon solemnly asked his audience, still reading and wondering himself what the answer was going to be. "Why, my dear reader, every time Simon pinched them, they squealed! You can't be more *real* than that!"

Simon smiled when he looked up from his book to see Sylvia and Isadore Green holding out their arms to him, waiting to be pinched.

CHAPTER 7
Universal Knowledge

"Wait a minute!" Isadore interjected when they finally stopped pinching and squealing and giggling. "I forgot to put in that biography what made Simon Green so smart. He never listens to the radio! Not even once! Can't believe I forgot to put that in!"

"It is true," Simon replied, nodding his head up and down solemnly. "Much money was needed for a radio, and we did not have much money. Effie and Hans did not have a radio either. But I thought American children did much radio listening. On the ship the American children spoke of many programs they knew."

"And were those children very bright? No, they

were not! Radio listening corrupts the mind and kills the imagination!" Isadore Green announced as if he were speaking at an anti-radio rally. "Reading . . . that's the pathway to knowledge, the only pathway! Books! Newspapers! Magazines! Almanacs! Read, don't listen!" He grabbed up a book and flipped its pages.

"I'm afraid Izzy's a real radical on some subjects," Sylvia told Simon under her breath. "A radical is a person who . . . well . . ."

"And another reason Simon Green is so smart," Isadore interrupted, "is that he has read *The Encyclopedia Britannica: A New Survey of Universal Knowledge* from start to finish. Not once, but several times!"

"I have read what?" Simon asked, turning to Sylvia with a question mark on his face.

"That was the present we were about to give you," Sylvia explained. "Before your . . . father," Sylvia skipped over the word quickly, "ran off the track and felt compelled to scare the wits out of you by telling you why you must forget your past—"

"Sylvie! We have settled the question of Simon's past. There are some secrets that must be kept. Some things never to be discussed. If it will make you feel better, we'll make a game out of it for Simon. You like games, don't you, Simon? You said you liked that little thumbs-up game."

Simon propped his thumbs up in the air and nodded his head. Isadore had asked him that question yesterday. Yesterday, when he was Simon Singer.

"Well," Isadore Green went on, "we'll just turn the rules around and call our new game 'Simon *Doesn't* Say.' Simon doesn't say anything about his life before he came to Pennsylvania. Simon doesn't say any German words, doesn't even *think* German words!"

"Not even *Gesundheit*?" Simon asked, lowering his eyes to the floor and sticking his lip out once more. "Hannah taught me to always say *Gesundheit* when somebody sneezed."

"Not even *that*," Izzy replied in his icicle voice.

Simon thought he heard Sylvia, who was standing behind him, crying softly, but he didn't turn around. This was a play, and he was acting a part. The boy acting the part of the son didn't have to feel real sorrow for the mother, did he? She seemed to be a very nice lady, but he didn't have to feel real sorrow for her. Not like he felt real sorrow for his Polish grandmother when the Nazis took her away.

Suddenly, with the flourish of a magician unveiling a missing assistant, Isadore Green pulled a sheet off of a long line of books on the floor next to the wall. The books, which had been arranged upright between two dog statue bookends, looked like uniformed soldiers lined up for inspection.

"Happy birthday to our new son, Simon Green!" Isadore called out like a circus ringmaster.

Simon's mouth dropped open and his eyes sparkled. He wasn't sure which he loved more, the books or the dog-shaped bookends that held them.

"We have all the time in the world to Americanize you, Simon, but since we're pretty far from town and the library, we needed help. School's out for the summer, so we'll teach you at home with *The Encyclopedia Britannica: A New Survey of Universal Knowledge* for our textbooks. We'll see how we feel about school when fall comes."

Simon had never seen such books. The rust-colored covers made the gold lettering appear three-dimensional. He set out to count them, ticking each volume off with his index finger. Twenty-four volumes! All the knowledge of the universe in twenty-four beautiful books! And they all belonged to him.

He started to explain that the Nazis had burned all his family's books, but he stopped his mouth before it betrayed him. No, he was not to talk of the past. He ran his fingers slowly down the row again, stopping to stroke each volume top to bottom as he went. His finger rippled back to the first one, which he slipped out and hugged to his chest.

Simon smiled at the mother. He was glad she had stopped crying. He watched as she walked over and took the father's hand. The mother. The father. *That's* how he could keep everything straight in his head! He was playing the part of the character named Simon Green. These people were characters, too. Isadore Green was *the* father and Sylvia Green was *the* mother. Not *his* mother or *his* father. When they did plays, Hannah always said, "I'll be *the* mother and you can be *the* father!"

He couldn't speak of them that way out loud, of course. That would not be proper English. But he could *think* of them that way. Sylvia Green was *the* mother. Isadore Green was *the* father. And he was Simon Green, *the* son.

"It's a fine birthday present, isn't it?" the mother said softly. "A fine present . . . for our new son."

"Until your reading of English improves, you can just look at the pictures and ask questions," Isadore explained. "When you've finished studying every page in the set very carefully, we'll get you a dog! In fact, we'll get a very smart dog, and he can teach you how to read." He laughed. "What do you think of that idea?"

"I think I must start looking at my books right now!" Simon cried as he threw himself on his stomach, propped his elbows on the floor, and cracked open the first volume. A few minutes passed before he looked up again, but Isadore and Sylvia didn't interrupt him, nor did they leave the room.

"I am going to need a bit of help, I think," he finally admitted.

Isadore slid the pillow from the overstuffed chair onto the floor beside Simon and motioned Sylvia to take a seat. "You get first shift," he said. "When your bottom gets tired, I'll take over! Remember, we have all the time in the world." He paused before he added, "Don't we, Sylvie? Tell me we've got all the time in the world."

Without waiting for her answer, he grabbed up his pipe, walked out the back screen door, and headed for the grove of trees that rimmed the house.

"Your ... your father loves trees," Sylvia explained. "Goes to them whenever he has thinking to do, whenever he has a problem to solve. He says they give him comfort. He's even got names for them!"

Simon watched him go, squinting his eyes so he could see as far as possible. Then, still squinting, he turned to look at Sylvia again, trying to determine if the expression on her face was happy or sad. She pulled him up from the floor and led him into the kitchen where the light was better. She took his chin in her hand and peered into his eyes as if she were searching for a loose eyelash.

"Simon," she said, drawing out his name very slowly, "have you ever had your eyes examined by a doctor who knew about eyesight?"

"It was not possible. Because of the Nazis. The Nazis did not want Jews to go to doctors. I wanted a doctor for Hannah, but it was not possible. I will be a doctor someday, so I can mend Hannah's leg. The Nazis only wanted rid of Jews. That was why they took my father—"

He stopped talking and put both hands over his mouth. He'd done it again—talked about the past. Now they would send him away ... take away his books ... he would never get his dog ...

"Oh, sweet Simon, it's all right! It's all right!" Sylvia cried, grabbing him in her arms and hugging him to her chest.

"You will not tell him I forgot, will you? I will not forget again! I promise you, I will not forget again! I am Simon Isadore Green! Don't let the Nazis find me! I am Simon Isadore Green!"

"Of course you are," she sobbed. "Of course you

are! And it will get easier, Simon. You will forget. Children forget very quickly. You will forget!" She dried her tears and his. "And we will get you to an eye doctor right away. If you are going to read all these books, you are going to need to see very, very well."

She sat down in a kitchen chair, pulled him onto her lap, and, as she had done the night before, began to hum to him.

"I'm sure Izzy's right, asking you to forget your past," she whispered when her song ended. "I was just surprised by all he said. Izzy often surprises me. But I see now. You are our son, our own precious son, and we cannot be too careful, cannot protect you enough. You will forget the sadness of your past soon, very soon."

The boy he was pretending to be nestled into the soft, warm lap of the mother, but Simon Singer could not erase the faces of his mother, his father, and Hannah from his head. His Polish grandmother was there, too. He did not *want* to forget his family, not even his father, who had signed papers and sent him away.

He had a picture of his family with him when he left Germany, a picture printed on the back of a post-card. His mother had slipped it inside *The Tale of*

Peter Rabbit and given it to him when she hugged him good-bye, when she told him, "You are our family's future, Simon." But in the scramble of disembarking, he had left both the book and the photograph on the ship, and the man named Max said there was no time to go back and look for them.

Simon wished for that picture now. To help him remember. But there was no way to get it back, no way at all. He folded his fingers into fists again, thumbs pointed toward the ceiling of the sunny yellow kitchen, and whispered so softly that not even the mother who held him could hear, "Don't forget Simon Singer! Don't forget Hannah! Don't forget!"

But because it was late and he was very tired, Simon Green forgot to say the all-important and necessary "Simon Says." And so, as the years slipped by, Simon Green forgot that he was acting, forgot that Sylvia and Isadore Green were *the* mother and *the* father. He only remembered that they were his parents and that he was their son.

Until he moved to Oklahoma and found that postcard.

On the very same day his best friend was moving away forever.

CHAPTER 8
Good-bye, John Alan Feester

August 3, 1942
Apache, Oklahoma

"Wave good-bye, Simon!" Rachel demanded. "John Alan's waving at you! Stop stomping those stupid ants and wave back at him!"

"I can't wave. Waving's not allowed. Somebody might think I was *Heil*-ing Hitler," Simon scoffed, but he didn't say it loud enough for Rachel to hear him.

"Wave, Simon! Wave!" Rachel screeched as she began to circle her arms around like the propeller on an airplane getting ready for takeoff.

"John Alan Feester's not nearly as smart as he thinks he is," Simon growled when he heard John Alan's father fire up the engine of the Buick and then saw him begin to back the car out of the driveway.

"Stop talking and stomping and start waving, Simon," Rachel pleaded. "John Alan's going to think you don't care he's leaving."

"I don't," Simon informed her. "I don't care at all. John Alan Feester is stupid, and I don't like stupid people." He watched long enough to see John Alan's car round the curve leading out of town, but then he went back to his ant stomping.

"What are you talking about, Simon? John Alan's not stupid. He may not have read the encyclopedia four times, but he's sure not stupid. What's got into you anyway?" Rachel asked, just before she burst into tears.

"Bet you my Captain Midnight Code-O-Graph badge he doesn't write us once," Simon muttered, but Rachel didn't reply. She was too busy crying and wiping her runny nose on her shirt-sleeve.

"Good grief, Rachel, can't you keep your nose clean?" Simon sneered, using John Alan's favorite admonition. He jerked his handkerchief out of his pocket and shoved it in her hand. "Blow!" he commanded, but just as she grabbed it, he suddenly remembered it was not *his* handkerchief, it was Simon Singer's handkerchief, the one he had taken from the tin box in the basement, the one with "S.S." embroidered on it!

"I need that handkerchief back," he said quickly. "Today. So don't snot it up!" He punctuated his demand with a stomp.

"Don't say *snot* to me, Simon Green! And quit stomping your feet! I'll give you your dumb handkerchief back when I'm good and ready!"

He needed to steer her away from the subject of the handkerchief before she started inspecting it to see what made it so important to him.

"I'll tell you just how stupid John Alan Feester is," he said. "He thinks the tribunal for those German saboteurs starts tomorrow! Nobody knows when it started, but I'm pretty sure it's going on right now! Those tribunals don't mess around like ordinary courts do. John Alan never reads the papers, does he? I started to correct him when he said that, but he's such a smart mouth know-it-all—"

"Stop talking bad about him like that, Simon! What are you so mad about anyway? You came out of that basement mad as a wet hen. It's not John Alan's fault he's having to move!"

"He won't even send us a postcard," Simon

goaded before he remembered he wasn't even ever going to *think* the word "postcard" again.

Rachel ignored his barb and clutched the handkerchief by the initialed corner. The letters were so tiny, she didn't even notice them. Simon tried not to look at that long forgotten part of his past, but he couldn't help himself. How could he have been so stupid as to give it to her?

"Why do we care whether he writes or not?" Simon prodded. "John Alan's nothing but a belligerent enigma! I heard you call him that yourself, and you were right! I'm glad he's gone."

Maybe John Alan Feester *had* been his best friend, but he wasn't anymore. Simon Green would simply forget him. Just like he'd forgotten all those other people who had been part of his life.

Until today. Until he had found out they were hungry.

Just so John Alan would know he wasn't going to miss him, Simon had marched to the center of the ant bed and started stomping right in the middle of John Alan's good-bye to him. He hadn't said a word, hadn't even replied when John Alan asked him a question.

And now John Alan was gone.

Out of sight.

Forever.

But Simon Green couldn't stop stomping.

"Stop stomping those ants, Simon! They've got to be pulverized by now," Rachel commanded.

"Pulverized" was her word for the day, she had informed them while they waited for John Alan's father to finish loading the trunk of the car. Rachel's father, the editor of *The Apache Republican* newspaper, made her learn a new word every day. Then she had to use it three times. Simon and John Alan liked using big words, too, but they didn't make a big *deal* about it like Rachel did.

"I said stop *pulverizing* those ants," Rachel repeated, holding up two fingers. She jerked her glasses off and tried to rub away the tear stains with the handkerchief, but that smudged her lenses even more. "Push your specs back up your nose before they slide off and get smashed flat as those poor ants," she ordered.

Simon, still keeping track of his handkerchief out of the corner of his eyes, shoved his glasses back up his nose and ran the fingers of both hands through his sweaty hair. He didn't, however, stop his stomping, even though his toothpicky legs were getting very tired.

"Why you talking ugly about John Alan, anyway,

Simon? Why'd you say he won't write us? Of course he'll write! He's gotta let us know what he's doing, doesn't he? And furthermore, I haven't called him a belligerent enigma once this year. Not since you moved here and made us stop fighting all the time. Going back to California's not gonna change the way John Alan feels about us. He promised to write to us forever."

"Forever's a very long time, Rachel," Simon grunted. "Nothing lasts forever. Believe me, I know."

"Love does," Rachel countered. She was glad Simon was too busy stomping to notice the blush that covered her face when she said the word "love" and remembered the kiss John Alan gave her before he jumped in the car to leave. It was her first real kiss ever, and it was right on the lips! Simon had been too busy stomping to see it. She was glad about that, too.

"Letters last forever, too," she prattled, "if you save 'em and tie 'em up with a ribbon. My Gram has every letter my Gunny ever wrote her. All tied up with blue ribbons. She keeps them in a trunk in her basement so nothing can hurt them! Not even a tornado!"

Trunk? Basement? Simon contemplated why Rachel never stopped prying into people's private thoughts. She was always bringing up private topics that should never be discussed, topics like trunks and basements. The next thing he knew, she'd be asking him if he knew any people who were hungry. Simon began to chew on the inside of his cheek in rhythm to his stomping.

"Remember that quote about letters?" Rachel rambled on. "The one Miss Cathcart put on the blackboard last year? Right after Joe Bob Snow got sent overseas? When she wrote him every single day?" As she always did when she mentioned Joe Bob and Miss Cathcart, who were now Private First Class and Mrs. Joe Bob Snow, Rachel rolled her eyes and sighed. She sighed again, louder this time, as she recited, "'Letters mingle souls; For thus friends absent speak.'" Out of the corner of his eye Simon saw her wave his handkerchief in the air like Juliet signaling from the balcony. "Can't remember who *said* that," she admitted, "but I think it's simply beautiful."

"Nobody *said* it, Rachel," Simon muttered, wishing he could jerk that handkerchief right out of her hand. "John Donne *wrote* those words. In a letter. To Sir Henry Wotton. Around 1602."

Simon, who had an almost photographic memory, couldn't help spouting names and dates like that, even when he was stomping ants. He tried not to sound like a know-it-all showoff, but he had so many facts rolling around his head he had to empty them out from time to time. Especially on a day like this, when so many bad things were happening, so many bad memories surfacing. Reciting facts kept him from thinking about other things, things like basements and trunks and postcards.

"Well, my daddy says letters are the lifeline of the military, even if they do get censored," Rachel rattled. "My mama couldn't make any sense out of Uncle Claude's last one. I put it up to the window and squinted at those blacked-out words for over an hour! Couldn't read one single letter."

"Well, John Alan's not in the military, so nobody'll censor his letter. *If* he ever gets around to writing one." Simon examined the ground below his feet as if it were a blackboard where he was doing a complicated arithmetic problem. If he could just stay mad at John Alan, he wouldn't have to miss him. It had worked with Bernard Singer, hadn't it?

"Since Los Angeles is approximately one thousand three hundred forty-seven miles from here, it might take John Alan and his father a whole week to get there. Especially if they have a flat tire or can't find filling stations." He bit his lip before he added, "That's longer than it took Mother and me to get here from Pennsylvania. But that was before Pearl Harbor. Before lower speed limits. Before War Time." He looked up from the ground and into Rachel's brown eyes that were studying him carefully. "John Alan won't even remember what we look like by the time he gets to California." Simon continued to punctuate his conversation with first his right foot, then his left in what was beginning to look like a jitterbug dance he never intended to stop. "A ... really ... long ... time ..." Four more stomps.

Even though it was hard to tell through those pop-bottle-thick lenses of his, Rachel was pretty sure she could see tears rimming Simon's eyes, the only eyes in the world weaker than hers. Every year their mothers sent them off to school with notes requesting front row desks, a real humiliation—especially since they were entering sixth grade, the top class in Theodore Roosevelt Elementary, this fall.

Rachel pretended to cough so she could bend her head and check out his face more closely. Sure enough, one lone tear was tracing a path through the ant bed dust on his right cheek. She started to give him his handkerchief back, but if she did, he'd know she'd seen the tear, so she stuffed it in her pocket and glanced away before he caught her looking again.

Rachel had never seen Simon cry, not even when

they heard that Joe Bob Snow had been killed in the Battle of Midway. Joe Bob was the best friend of Rachel's big brother, Al, and Mr. Snow, his grandfather, was the school janitor. All the kids, girls *and* boys, too, bawled their eyes out the day Miss Pevehouse, the librarian, took Joe Bob's picture off the red, white, and blue bulletin board with "THEY PROUDLY SERVE" across the top. She put the picture in a gold frame and arranged it in the trophy case in the middle of all the gold footballs on shiny wooden bases the team won when Joe Bob was their quarterback.

Rachel and John Alan tried to avoid the trophy case after that, because Joe Bob's picture made them want to cry every time they saw it. But not Simon Green. Simon marched right by that case several times a day and never once batted an eyelash, damp or dry.

Later on, when it turned out a mistake had been made—a humongous, enormous, huge, gigantic mistake—and Joe Bob wasn't really dead after all, every single person in Apache, population 1,938, cried again. But this time they cried because they were happy—happy Joe Bob had come home alive, happy because he and Miss Cathcart got married, happy because the Snow family was happy. Everybody cried.

But not Simon Green. Sad or happy either one, Simon never cried.

"You might as well face it, Rachel. We'll never lay eyes on John Alan Feester again. Not ever."

"Look, Simon," Rachel replied, "lots of people who move away come back. At least for a visit anyway. Sometimes they even come back for good! Look at Paul. He moved to California New Year's Day, and here it is only August, and he's moving back home already. Maybe that'll happen to John Alan, too! I hope so. It hurts something awful to lose your best friend. I thought I'd die the day Paul moved. It's the absolute worst thing that can ever happen in the history of the world! Believe me, I know! I've suffered!"

Simon gave her a look that chilled her, even though the August sun had shoved the whole state of Oklahoma into a red-hot oven and slammed the door on the panhandle.

"You got no idea what you're talking about, Rachel. You don't know the *first* thing about losing people, not the first thing!" His voice snapped and stung her like a jar full of those ants he was annihilating. "Not ... anything ... at ... all!"

Suddenly, his feet stopped moving and his legs stayed straight, and he and Rachel both stared down at the ant bed. What had been a big volcano of dark red dirt when he launched his attack now lay flat and empty as a pin-pricked balloon. It seemed impossible that a single ant, above or below ground, could have survived his onslaught.

"Why'd you do that, Simon?" Rachel blurted out. "Why'd you stomp those poor old ants to death? They weren't bothering anybody way out here. I thought you liked ants. That ant farm of yours won the grand prize in the science fair last year. You told John Alan and me those ants were your pets! Why'd you want to kill all of these?"

Simon kept his eyes on the flattened bed quite a while before he finally raised them to stare at her. It was even longer before he spoke, but Rachel bit her tongue and waited.

"You have lived in the very same house, in the very same town, with the very same father, and the very same mother, and the very same brother, your whole very same life, haven't you, Rachel Elizabeth Very Same Dalton?" Simon shot the words out in such rapid, machine-gun-fire order, he had to stop to catch his breath several times before his question ended. But he didn't say anything at all about the ants.

Rachel's head bobbed up and down like a wind-up doll as she watched his mouth, listened to this voice, and tried to understand what he was talking about. She had asked him about killing the *ants*, but Simon was talking about *her*. And her mother. And father. And Al.

"You've even had the very same name all your very same life, haven't you?" Simon pressed on. This time he waited for an answer.

"What a dumb question, Simon. I've never known anybody who changed their name, except for girls when they got married. And then there was Edward Lee Jordon, whose name used to be Austin Leon Fraizer before he got adopted, and they—" She stopped in midsentence, put her tongue between her teeth, and bit down on it very hard.

Simon clenched his jaw and narrowed his eyes at her. He knew the minute John Alan was gone Rachel would bring up the subject of adoption! She *always* wanted to pry into private matters. Girls were like that, even his mother. Always wanting to know your private business, always wanting to know what you were thinking.

John Alan knew how to shut Rachel up when she brought up subjects they didn't want to talk about, subjects like adoption. John Alan had shut her up a bunch of times when she mentioned that subject. Now that he was gone, who was going to keep her from asking all her questions?

Besides, his being adopted didn't have a single thing to do with what was happening to him now. Isadore and Sylvia Green were his *real* parents. He wasn't just acting like he was their son. He *was* their son, and they were his father and his mother. Not *the* father and *the* mother like characters in a play, but *his* father and *his* mother in real life—in his real life!

He'd had to make up a bunch of adoption stories when Miss Cathcart asked him in front of the whole class when his birthday was. He couldn't tell the truth because the father ... *his* father ... made him promise to forget the past, to never give out any information about his past to anybody.

The truth was Simon was a Jew, and his mother and father were Jews, even though they all kept it a secret. Hitler was looking for Jews—looking hard. Those German saboteurs the FBI had captured were proof of that. They had been sent to America to burn Jewish businesses. It said so in the newspaper! That was why he was so worried about them, so worried about *everything* now that he'd seen that postcard and remembered he had once been Simon Singer.

"I mean ... I mean ..." Rachel was stammering like John Alan had just poked her in the ribs. "Changing your name like Edward Lee had to do is not a *bad* thing to have happen. I've wished about a zillion times I could change my name. The ... the Elizabeth part, I mean, so my initials wouldn't spell *red*. Those initials have made my life pretty miserable!"

Simon couldn't stand her whining about stupid things one more minute. Rachel Elizabeth Dalton and her miserable life! She didn't have hungry people sending her postcards begging her to send them something to eat. She wasn't worried that Nazi saboteurs might be looking for her. She didn't have a sister who might be ... who might be ...

He needed to shut her up like John Alan used to do.

"How about having S.S. for your initials, Rachel Elizabeth Dalton?" he shouted, even though she was standing right in front of him. "Try those initials on for size! Slip your feet into a pair of shiny black jackboots and goosestep in them! S.S. ... as in Nazis! S.S. ... as in swastika! S.S. ... as in Hitler! S.S. ... as in *Schultastaffel*! Why don't ya make *Schultastaffel* your word for the day? S.S.! That's what *my* initials will be again if those hungry people find me!"

He peered at her over the top of his glasses as he pulled back one leg and then the other to kick dirt and dead ants all over her bare feet. He stopped short of stomping her toes. Getting her toes stomped would teach her a good lesson, he thought, but he couldn't go that far.

"Good grief, Simon, have you gone crazy? What's wrong with you? What are you talking about? Hitler? Swastika? S.S.? Nazi? What's any of that got to do with you or me or those ants?" She swiped one foot over the top of the other, trying to wipe the dirt and gravel off her feet without using her hands, since she could see now that some of the ants were still alive and wiggling.

Simon didn't reply. He jumped off the ant bed and put both hands over his face, palms out, as if she had just slapped him in the mouth.

"Simon ... I don't know why I said that ... I'm really sorry I mentioned adoption again. John Alan warned me ... I'm really, really sorry. But what you just said about Nazis, about the S.S.—"

"Well, I just don't think a stupid girl who has never moved in her life, has never had to change her name, never had to leave everything behind, has never ..." He grabbed her by both shoulders and squeezed them tight. "The mother and the father are the only parents I ever had, Rachel! I'm Simon Green, their only son! I'm not acting! Don't you ever say the word 'adopted' to me again!"

Simon stopped talking and started running, running as fast as he could, right down the middle of the street. The slowest runner in the fifth grade, the last person in line every recess, was now pounding his feet on the pavement the same way he'd pounded those ants. Only this time he was moving forward instead of up and down. Rachel had no idea he could run like that.

"Hannah! Bernard! Esther!" Simon cried out as he ran. "Effie!" he added, but the hot August air caught the names and shoved them all back down his throat.

"Simon Green, you come back here right this minute!" Rachel screamed. When he didn't obey, she took off running after him.

"Where in tarnation do you think you're going?" she hollered as loudly as she could. "Tarnation" was Paul's favorite word, but since it meant "damnation," Rachel wasn't allowed to use it. This was a terribly desperate situation, though, and terribly desperate situations called for strong language.

"Tarnation, tarnation, tarnation, Simon! I want to know what you're talking about!" she called out, but Simon had rounded the corner and disappeared.

And he hadn't even remembered to get his handkerchief back.

CHAPTER 9
Hello, Kenneth Stumbling Bear

Rachel turned to walk back to her bike when the hot griddle of pavement suddenly reminded her she didn't have on any shoes. She hopped onto the weed-filled shoulder and landed right in the middle of an enormous sticker patch. Dancing around like a puppet with its leg strings broken, she was about to burst out crying when she heard a familiar voice calling her name.

"Rachel? That you? Stay where you are! Stop jumping up and down! You're just giving those stickers more bull's-eyes to hit!"

She turned a complete circle before she spotted

Kenneth Stumbling Bear at the corner of the sidewalk that led to John Alan's now empty house. Kenneth, Paul's good friend and fellow artist, was pulling a big green and red wagon. In the wagon sat his little brother, Gus. Rachel watched as Kenneth lifted Gus out, placed him gently on the ground, and drew a big circle around him with a stick.

"Now, that's your very own tepee, little brother," she heard Kenneth say. "Don't go outside that circle till I come back for you. Lots of bears around here," he added, tugging one of the little boy's shiny black braids. Gus, who was four, plopped down, picked up the stick his brother had dropped, and began to draw a horse in the dirt.

Kenneth jogged toward Rachel, who was now standing on tiptoes trying to keep her heels from collecting any more stickers than were already in the balls of her feet. Simon's amazing outburst took a temporary back seat to her current dilemma as she watched the wagon bounce up and down on the uneven ground. Since it was the largest one Radio Flyer made, it didn't tip over.

"That fire on your head can be seen for miles," Kenneth confided in a tone used by spies in the movies. "Gus and me, we spotted it clear over at the Legion Hut, where we were unloading our newspapers. Figured you were sending a smoke signal. Hop in my wagon and trusty Kiowa brave will rescue *aulgulmagaun* from deadly sticker patch!" Kenneth didn't crack a smile as he imitated the way Hollywood Indians talked in the movies. When "stoic" was her word for the day, Rachel used it all three times to describe Kenneth because he was so good at keeping a straight face.

"I gotta know what *aulgulmagaun* means first!" Rachel said, grinning as she narrowed her eyes at him. "Paul told me your tricks! Teaching him Kiowa, telling him a word meant one thing when it really meant something else! What are you calling me, Kenneth?"

"Who *me*? Get Paul in trouble? Not me, *aulgulmagaun*! I'd never do that! *Aulgulmagaun* just means redheaded female in Kiowa. But since there aren't any redheaded Kiowas, female or otherwise, we don't get to use that word except when we're talking to hot-tempered white girls," he laughed as he turned to check on his brother. "Help me keep an eye on Gus, will you? His favorite game these days is 'run and hide.' He can escape faster than Harry Houdini. Hop in the wagon, Rachel!"

"Me? In a little kid's wagon?" she squealed. "I thought you were kidding! What if somebody from our class saw me? You gotta be crazy!"

"Crazy? If I was crazy, I'd be Stumbling Crazy Horse, not Crazy Stumbling Bear," he laughed.

"But ... a little kid's wagon, Kenneth," she said, screwing up her mouth and bouncing from foot to foot. "I'm eleven and a half years old almost. I can't—"

"Don't see cowboy on horse coming to save you, *nau:com*," Kenneth pointed out, again imitating a silver screen Indian as he held his fingers over his eyes and gazed off in the distance. "*Nau:com* is Kiowa for 'good friend.' Paul gave me a baseball card for every Kiowa word I taught him! You got two Kiowa words for nothing! *Aulgulmagaun* either got to ride in wagon of your *nau:com* Kenneth or run with the stickers!"

"Listen, Kenneth, *aulgulmagaun* has a problem worse than stickers! Something awful's wrong with Simon. Something to do with John Alan leaving ... or Simon being adopted ... or me never moving ..."

She stopped short of mentioning the part about the Nazis or the S.S. That part of Simon's outburst was so strange and scary, she wasn't sure she should tell anybody about it. Not yet, anyway. On the radio, Captain Midnight said there were spies, traitors, and saboteurs in every town. While she was certain Simon would not be one of those, if he knew something about the Nazis, about the S.S., then maybe ...

"We've got to help him, that's all," she said, looking down at her feet so she wouldn't have to look Kenneth in the eyes.

"Well, we gotta get you out of this sticker patch first. You're too heavy for me to carry, so you gotta get in my wagon." Kenneth pointed both of his index fingers at her and then at the bed of the Radio Flyer.

Rachel took a deep breath and climbed in over the side rails, sliding as far down below the wooden side-rail slats as she could.

"Roll me back over to John Alan's driveway fast," she begged. "That's where I left my bike, next to Gus' tepee." She put her head down on her knees and crossed her arms over her forehead to hide her face, even though she knew her red hair would give her away to anybody who saw her.

Kenneth grabbed the handle and began a slow jog over the bumpy terrain that led to the sidewalk.

"Why was Simon running like that?" he called over one shoulder. "Where was he going?"

"Got no idea. I'm about to decide he got heat stroke! Something seemed to snap in his head when John Alan got ready to leave. Simon jumped in the middle of a big ant bed and started stomping ants instead of telling John Alan good-bye. It was crazy!" Simon's words flashed through her mind like bolts of greased lightning. Nazi! Swastika! Hitler! S.S.! He'd yelled all those words! He had really yelled them at her. What was he talking about?

"I've ... I've read about soldiers getting heat stroke, Kenneth," she repeated. "It makes them crazy, and Simon is acting crazy. It's really, really hot today, so I think that must be what happened to him."

"If Simon had heat stroke, he couldn't run, Rachel. With heat stroke you're lucky if you can crawl. My Uncle Bob taught me about heat stroke. He's a doctor in the army now. Forty-fifth Division, pride of the Southwest once they got those swastika patches off their uniforms!"

Swastika! Simon Green had been yelling about swastikas. Why was Kenneth taking about swastikas now? Was there some connection? Something she didn't know about?

"What about swastikas, Kenneth? I know it's on the Nazi flag, but what's that got to do with your Uncle Bob and the army?"

Kenneth stopped pulling the wagon, dropped the handle, and whirled around to face her. His dark eyes were flashing. Rachel had never seen Kenneth mad, not once in the five whole years they'd been in school together.

"You mean you haven't heard about the swastika

and the Forty-fifth? The swastika was one of the most sacred Indian symbols ever, Rachel, except we called it the Whirling Log. It meant different things to different tribes—life to one, sun to another, even good luck! But it was always a real *powerful* sign, a life-giving sign! The swastika was *ours* till Hitler stole it! Stole it and *twisted* it to make it his sign. When Indians heard about that, we erased it from our lives. Some tribes even issued proclamations swearing that the swastika would never appear on anything they made or wore again!"

Rachel was staring at him with her mouth open. She'd never heard Kenneth talk that much in his whole life, and he wasn't through yet.

"Since there were lots of Indians in the Forty-fifth, the whole division wore swastika patches on their uniforms. But because of Adolph Hitler, they had to change the swastika to a thunderbird. They did that three years ago, before half the world knew how awful Hitler really is. My grandmother made her fingers bleed sewing new patches on Uncle Bob's uniforms." He shook his head as he picked up the wagon handle and began to pull again. "It's a sorry world when a *qahiaulkaui Hitleroba* can ruin a sacred symbol. *Qahiaulkaui Hitleroba* ... that's Kiowa for Hitler. It means crazy madman!"

"I never heard that story, Kenneth. That's awful! I don't blame you for being mad about it. Maybe *that's* what Simon was yelling about. Whatever it was, it sure had him talking crazy, and I've got to find out why."

The wagon rolled to a stop.

"Well, here we are, *aulgulmagaun*, back in civilization again." He swiped two fingers over her hair, and then jerked his hand back and blew on them as if he had burned himself. "You lucky we good friends. I could trade that rare red scalp of yours for many fine blankets!"

"Some talent scout driving through here's gonna hear you talking like a genuine simulated Injun and carry you off to Hollywood. Star you in a John Wayne movie," Rachel giggled as she slid to a sitting position. Kenneth could always make her smile, even on an awful day like this one.

She grabbed the wagon's side rails, preparing to make the fastest exit possible, when she heard the frantic ringing of a bicycle bell followed by the screeching voice of Agnes Ann Billingsly.

"Boy, you must be hard up for a ride, Rachel!" Agnes Ann shouted as she zipped up on her bike and began to circle Kenneth's wagon like a hungry buzzard. "Rachel's got a boyfriend! A redskin boyfriend," she yelled before she took off again.

"Redskin boyfriend!" Gus shouted happily from his ringside seat in the tepee circle. Kenneth looked at him and shook his head slowly.

"Why, that snot-nosed twit—" Rachel began, but Kenneth put his hand over her mouth.

"Twit! Twit! Twit!" Gus echoed, beating his stick on the picture he'd drawn on the ground.

"Little pitchers have big ears," Kenneth cautioned. "Anyway, Gus is too young to understand. Grandmother and I will explain it to him. When the time comes. Sorry to say there's lots of Agnes Anns in the world."

"But Kenneth!" Rachel cried, stamping her foot before she remembered she still had sticker trouble. "Tarnation!" she hollered at top decibel.

"Tarnation!" Gus repeated gleefully.

"I got to get this baby away from here before you ruin him for tribal living," Kenneth told her, stifling the grin threatening to break across his face.

"I not a baby!" Gus informed him stoutly as he transformed his drawing stick into a javelin and flung it at his brother's kneecap.

"Oh, no you don't!" Kenneth hollered just as Gus sprang up like a jack-in-the-box and sprinted off down the street toward town hollering "Bear! Bear!"

"Gotta go, Rach. See you later!" Kenneth grabbed the handle of the wagon and took off after his brother.

Rachel jumped on her bike, winced when another sticker jabbed into her foot, and took off for home. She wished Agnes Ann had stuck around long enough for Rachel to tell her exactly "how the cow ate the cabbage."

That old saw of Paul's grandpa popped into her head as she pedaled past the house where the old man used to live. "I'll tell them Republicans exactly 'how the cow ate the cabbage!'" Mr. Griggs often yelled as he crumpled up the newspaper and pounded his cane on the porch railing for an exclamation point. He'd been dead a whole year, but Rachel still imagined she could hear that cane banging as she went by.

She couldn't wait for Paul to get back from California. He'd know how to get the truth out of Simon Green. There wasn't anything Paul Griggs couldn't do!

CHAPTER 10

The Truth of the Trees

The minute he pushed off of his ant hill starting block, leaving Rachel screaming in the dust, Simon knew the track meet he had just entered would end in the grove of trees known as Daddy Warbucks' mansion on the playground of Roosevelt Elementary School. That's where he always headed when he needed to trade his pain for someone else's. It was a trick he'd learned in that grove of trees in Pennsylvania the first summer Simon Singer began to play the part of Simon Green.

Simon Green thought he'd locked Simon Singer up in that tin box in the basement, but Simon Singer had escaped somehow—escaped and sneaked upstairs to reveal himself to Rachel. Simon Green knew, though, that once he reached the trees, Simon Singer couldn't overpower him again because by the time he reached the trees, he wouldn't *be* Simon Green anymore. He'd be Glenn Cunningham!

As he neared the grove, he imagined a yellow finish line tape stretched taut between the two trees that anchored the southwest corner. He bent his arms and put his hands up chest high, fingers spread, and felt the sweet sting of victory as his palms broke the ribbon! Glenn Cunninghan had just won the first-place medal in the mile race, and his time of 4:24.7 had set an interscholastic high school track record!

Simon threw both arms up in triumph and then crumpled to the ground. He knew that the real Glenn Cunningham, who *had* set that record as a high school senior, wouldn't have stopped to rest like that. The real Cunningham would have needed to run more laps because his burn-scarred legs hurt so much when they stopped moving. But Simon Green's legs had never been burned, and since he was only playing the part of Glenn Cunningham, he could enjoy the famous runner's record-setting win without having to endure any of his pain. That was the wonderful thing about becoming other people.

When he regulated his breathing again, Simon

rolled over on his back, stretched out his arms and legs, and squinted at the blue sky filtering through the leaves of the four horse apple trees that surrounded him. Nubby, lime-green horse apples dotted the spider-web pattern of the trees' umbrella-like branches. A burst of August wind knocked one of them to the hard, dusty ground beside him. He picked it up and began to drop it back and forth from one hand to the other as he remembered the first time he came to this place on a cold January day last winter.

Rachel had brought him here when they finished their lunch, and John Alan had come along, too. The four trees had been planted in the shape of a miniature baseball diamond, and the moment Simon saw the area inside, he realized the wonderful possibilities. The space inside those trees could be the infield of Yankee stadium, the ballroom of a grand hotel, the stage of a marvelous movie theater, even the office of the president of the United States! But Rachel, as always, had her own ideas.

"Simon," she had announced, sweeping the air with one arm, "I give you Daddy Warbucks' mansion, home of the irrepressible Little Orphan Annie!" Since "irrepressible" was her word for the day, she stuck one finger in the air and rolled her eyes before she added, "Paul named it when we were in first grade. The roots sticking up out of the ground marked off rooms, so we decided it was the mansion Little Orphan Annie got to live in after Daddy Warbucks adopted her!"

Simon remembered the evil eye John Alan had given Rachel when she blurted out the word "adopted" just one hour after Miss Cathcart had made Simon admit *he* was adopted. In front of the whole class. But Rachel was so busy explaining why the mansion belonged to her, she didn't even notice she'd brought up a very *touchy* subject. Her own father, she informed them, had dug up one of these trees when it was a sapling. Dug it up from the bank of Cache Creek, wrapped it in a burlap bag, and dragged it all the way to the schoolyard to plant it. That was why the mansion was her very own private playhouse.

"President Theodore Roosevelt rode the train to Oklahoma once a month to water these four saplings to be sure they lived!" she added without an ounce of shame for her lie. "He went to all that trouble because he was so happy our school had been named for him!"

Simon had started to point out the impossibility of such a statement since Roosevelt, who assumed the presidency on September 14, 1901, due to the assassination of William McKinley, would have hardly had the time to worry about a bunch of horse apple trees down in Oklahoma Territory. But he realized then and there that Rachel's imagination was as vivid as his own, so he decided to join her flights of fancy and let Daddy Warbucks' mansion be his stage, too.

He had enjoyed playing President Franklin Delano Roosevelt there and not having to endure the pain of polio. He had gloried in hitting home runs right out of those trees just like Lou Gehrig and not having to get that awful disease. Since John Alan and Rachel were the only audience he ever entertained other than his mother, most of his acting had been done right here in this spot, right where he was sitting now.

Suddenly, he jumped up and bowed, imagining that John Alan was giving him a standing ovation. Then Simon remembered that John Alan was never going to applaud him again, so he erased his memory from his mind and sat back down again.

Simon sighed as Rachel's brother zipped by on his bicycle, a package of meat from Mr. Schwartz's market bouncing in his basket. Al, who delivered for most of the stores in town now that gas was about to be rationed, flashed him the "V for Victory" sign. Simon signaled him back and hollered, "Kick the Krauts!"

As he watched Al disappear, Simon wished for the hundredth time that he had been able to bring his bicycle to Oklahoma. Losing his bike, his dog, and his father all at the same time was a triple blow, but the tiny moving van they had to rent because of wartime shortages filled up quickly. His mother had promised him a new bike, a Schwinn this time, but then Pearl Harbor was bombed, and no more bikes were being made for The Duration.

"Hey, there, Miss Orphan Annie," Simon drawled to the treetops in his best John Wayne voice, "you know about The Duration, honey? The time between when this dad-gum war started and when it will end? You don't? Well, let me tell you, I'm dad-gum tired of the dad-blamed Duration!" He looked around a moment to be sure nobody was riding by before he added, "Damn The Duration! Double damn The Duration!"

Simon enjoyed cussing. He wasn't sure why, but cussing always made him feel better. His mother didn't allow him to do it, of course, but he couldn't help the way the people he was playing talked, and some of them, like John Wayne, cussed a lot.

Staying mad at John Alan made him feel better, too. *Stupid* John Alan, who had agreed to Rachel's stupid letter writing plan!

"You can write one letter to me and Kenneth and Paul and Simon!" she announced the day they found out John Alan was moving. "That way you'll write more often, and you'll save paper and postage money. Besides, we don't have any secrets. We tell each other everything! Paul wrote his letters that way and so can you."

Simon scowled. Rachel might think he and John Alan didn't have secrets from her, but she was wrong about that. They had their secrets, lots of them in fact. If Paul had really been her very best friend, she should have written him personal letters! Simon had told her that, but she wouldn't listen. He couldn't believe John Alan had agreed to do it that way, but he had. One more reason to forget him. Forget him the same way he'd forgotten the rest of them, even those people who were hungry.

Thinking of the hungry people caused Simon's stomach to growl, so he got up to start the trek home. He decided that after lunch he'd give Rachel a call, to see if she wanted to come over and listen to "Captain Midnight" with him. She'd talked John Alan and him both into joining the Captain's Secret Squadron, and the three of them had listened to the program together almost every weekday since they'd become friends.

This would be the first time he'd ever had to listen by himself since he had the measles back in January. That was when his mother had broken his father's rule forbidding radio listening and allowed Simon to borrow a set from Rachel's family since he couldn't read anything for three whole weeks.

After his mother started listening to the news with him every day, it was easy to talk her into letting him get his own radio, but he was on his honor as a Lone Scout to listen for only one hour a day.

If he did ask Rachel to come over, though, she'd want to cross-examine him about all those things he'd screamed at her, all those subjects he'd promised his father to never think or talk about again. But he hadn't been able to keep from saying the things he'd said. Seeing Simon Singer's name on that postcard, finding the handkerchief with "S.S." on it, worrying about the saboteurs, remembering his first days in America ... All of that, stacked right on top of John Alan moving away, had jerked the lid off Simon Green's personal Pandora's box and allowed all his troubles to escape at the same time.

Maybe if he let some time go by before he saw her again, Rachel would forget some of the things he said. If she did bring it up, he could always tell her he had just been acting, pretending to be a person who had seen the Nazis up close, a German citizen who'd lost his home to Hitler's henchmen. He could say he saw a person like that in the newsreels at the picture show. He could tell her he was acting, that's all. Just acting. That would work! He just needed to avoid her for a few days, give her time to forget what he yelled at her.

As he trudged up the sidewalk to his front porch, Simon saw his mother straightening the star flag in their window. She did that a lot lately. He ducked behind the hedge so she couldn't see him and bit his lip when he saw her carefully brush off what little dust the flag might have acquired since its last adjustment. He stared at the blue star in the middle of the white field, the blue star that meant someone they loved was serving their country. The blue star that would be turned to gold if the person they loved was killed. Then he did something Simon Singer had done so often, but that Simon Green had never even done once. He made fists with both of his hands, stuck his thumbs up in the air, and whispered, "Simon says, 'Dad, come home!'"

Simon and his mother had been in the crowd that watched Mr. and Mrs. Moran take down the blue star flag in their window and replace it with a gold one when their son, Wendell, got killed. The men from the American Legion wore their Legion hats, stood at attention, and saluted while Rachel's brother, Al, who played the trumpet in the high school band, played "Taps," and everybody cried. Everybody but Simon.

When his mother let the curtain drop, he waited a couple of minutes before going in.

"Madam Green," he intoned solemnly as he strolled in the door and swept up his violin from the bench where he had left it after last night's practice. "Allow me to introduce myself. I am the great Jascha Heifetz, violin virtuoso, come to play tunes on my fiddle with you if only you could grant me a few minutes of your precious time."

"Sorry, Jascha," she replied, quickly wiping her eyes with the back of one hand. "I've got something on the stove. Maybe next time you're in the neighborhood."

Simon sighed and put the violin back in its case. It had been a whole week since she'd played with him, her longest silence since his father left, and he missed her music.

But he missed his father much, much more.

CHAPTER 11
Simon's Secrets

"Agnes Ann Billingsly is a twit!" Rachel announced at the supper table as she scooped her mashed potatoes into the shape of an ant hill and dotted it with raisins from her bread pudding as a memorial to the ants. Three whole days had passed since Simon's mysterious outburst, and she hadn't laid eyes on him yet. She checked Daddy Warbucks' all the time, but the only person she'd seen around there was Agnes Ann Billingsly, who always took off like a Fourth of July skyrocket when Rachel rode by.

"A really, really big twit!" she repeated when her first statement drew no response.

"Now, Rachel," her mother cautioned, spooning

the raisins out of the mashed potato mountain and returning them to Rachel's pudding bowl, "I don't think 'twit' is a proper table word. It's British, isn't it? I'm never sure about that slang of theirs. Besides, I've told you time and again poor little Agnes Ann is to be pitied, not looked down upon. It's not her fault her father is thought to be a black marketeer. She's just—"

"Mean!" Rachel interjected. "Mean just like her daddy! She's also despicable, nefarious, contemptible, and infamous!" she added, using every word for the day she could think of that described Agnes Ann.

"This is all your fault, you know," her mother said, shaking her finger at Mr. Dalton. "You and your word for the day, dictionary-in-every-room mentality. And Rachel, an eleven-year-old child like Agnes Ann hasn't lived long enough to become infamous!"

"But Mama, it's true! She is! She called Kenneth a redskin! In front of Gus, too! Agnes Ann Billingsly's nothing but a snot-nosed—"

"Now there's a graphic 'word for the day' for you," Al joined in, pointing his fork at Rachel and grinning broadly. "Snot-nosed is right up there next to bugger face or—"

"Children! May I remind you again that we are

at the table? We do not refer to people in those terms at any time, but certainly not at the table!"

"Well, she is," Rachel insisted. "Snot-nosed, that is. She's never carried a handkerchief in her life! She just sticks her tongue out and licks."

"Rachel, you have tried our patience enough for one meal," Mr. Dalton broke in, narrowing his eyes at her. "Your mother had a bad day at the Red Cross. More orders for bandages than they can ever fill. If you insist on pursuing this particular topic of conversation, you may be excused from the table. Pass the Spam, please."

"Well, Daddy," Rachel said, ducking her head and smashing her mashed potato ant bed flat again, "then can I ask you just one question about Agnes Ann? Just one! Pretty please with sugar on it?"

"Sugar, as you well know, is being rationed now, Rachel, so a teaspoon-sized Agnes Ann question is all you get."

"Well, Agnes Ann's father is a bad person, and so is Agnes Ann, so—"

"Rachel, even though there are all kinds of rumors about Jake Billingsly, no charges have ever been brought against the man. In America, people are innocent until proven guilty, even German saboteurs who are caught red-handed."

"Well, I know that, and I also know there's no such thing as bad blood because you explained that to me, and John Alan told me the same thing when I asked him if he thought Simon might have bad blood because he was adopted, but—"

"Rachel Elizabeth Dalton!" her mother interrupted. "Why in the world would you ask a question like that? I swear, I don't know where you get such ideas! Certainly not from *my* side of the family! Sylvia Green is a wonderful mother, and Simon is an exceptional boy!"

"Well, I just wondered if maybe . . ."

"Listen to me, Rachel, Simon is Sylvia's son as much as Al is mine. He just happens to be adopted, that's all. The Greens care for their child just as much as your father and I care for the two of you. Sylvia said that when her husband joined the navy, he was so worried about leaving them he insisted they move to Oklahoma because he thought they'd be safer in the middle of the United States. Where they lived in Pennsylvania was very close to one of the country's biggest railroad centers, and Mr. Green was afraid it would be a prime target if this horrible war ends up on our very own soil."

"Isadore Green was right about that," Mr. Dalton agreed, reaching for the ketchup. "The FBI released a list of places those German saboteurs were headed, and sure enough Horseshoe Curve near Altoona and the Gallitzin Tunnel were on the list to be dynamited! Simon's mother told me those places were very close to where they lived. No wonder they wanted to get away from there. Smart man, Mr. Green. Great writer and really smart man."

"What do you think they'll do with those guys, Dad?" Al wanted to know.

"Electrocute them, I hope. And the sooner the better! That tribunal's been real hush-hush, but rumor has it Roosevelt will receive the verdict any time now, maybe tomorrow or Saturday."

"But it doesn't seem fair to kill the two guys that snitched! They helped the FBI find the rest of them, didn't they?"

"Very little about war is fair, son. I told you that when the brick got thrown through Sam Sing's window at the laundry on the day Pearl Harbor was bombed. All because his eyes are slanted, and because whoever threw that brick thought Sam was Japanese instead of Chinese. That wasn't fair at all.

"According to the FBI, thousands of Americans would've died if those German saboteurs had managed to poison the water supplies they were headed for. That wouldn't have been *fair* either. They were set to blow up Jewish businesses, create the same kind of panic they have all over Europe. Those men are Nazis, pure and simple, Nazis sent over here to show Americans that no place in the world is safe from Hitler's black-shirted thugs. We've got to show them they're wrong!"

"But could they execute them this week even? That's what I heard on the radio yesterday. That would sure be quick."

"Maybe. FDR followed the letter of the law. Made a proclamation. I put it in the paper, remember? Right before the Fourth. He asked for a Supreme Court ruling to see if a military tribunal could try them and got the okay right away. Yes, sir, I'm with Roosevelt all the way on this one, even if he is a Democrat! We have to make examples of those men, or we'll be at the mercy of every two-bit Nazi with a rubber raft and a paddle."

"Captain Midnight told us there were spies," Rachel informed her mashed potatoes, since none of the people at the table seemed interested in what she had to say. "Captain Midnight knows things are going to happen before they do. He knew about Pearl Harbor, remember? He's a very smart man. The FBI ought to listen to him, that's what I say!"

"Well, Punkin, I think the FBI did a pretty good

job without the help of your Captain. Those eight men only came in the last of June."

"Do you ... do you think they could come here? The Nazis, I mean?" Rachel asked, keeping her eyes on her plate. She had not said a word to anyone, certainly not her family, about what Simon screamed at her because she knew they'd accuse her of imagining things. It had happened before, like the time she decided John Alan Feester had something to do with the bombing of Pearl Harbor.

"Simon told me something ..." she went on, choosing her words very carefully. "I mean, Simon happened to be discussing the Nazis and S.S. and Hitler with me the other day. He said a lot of really strange things about them, and I was wondering if Simon maybe knew something that should ... should maybe ... maybe be reported to the FBI."

"As is often the case, you're not making much sense, Rachel. What kind of things did Simon say about the Nazis, and what prompted him to say them?" her father asked. "Pass the salt, please."

"Well, it was the day John Alan moved away, and Simon and I were telling him good-bye ... at least I was telling him good-bye. Simon was stomping a bunch of red ants so they wouldn't sting me since I didn't have any shoes on, and—"

"So *that's* how you got all those stickers!" her mother interrupted. "Rachel, I've told you and told you—"

"But Mama, Simon started stomping those ants because of me, but then he kept on and on and on! He couldn't stop stomping! It was like he wanted to kill every ant in the world! And then, when I reminded him that he really liked ants, that he had an ant farm of his own, all of a sudden he began to talk about you and Daddy and Al and me and how we had all lived in the same place our whole lives. Then he yelled at me, 'You don't know anything at all about losing people, Rachel! You never had to give up everything you loved!'"

"Well, that doesn't sound strange to me, Rachel," her mother said, spooning second helpings of mashed potatoes into every plate but hers. "Simon's father is off on a ship, and they have no idea where he is. Simon had to leave his dog back in Pennsylvania as well as all his relatives, and he—"

"But Mama, that's just it! He doesn't have any relatives in Pennsylvania. He told John Alan and me that one time."

"That's not unusual, either, Rachel," her father replied. "Not everybody's lucky enough to have family close by like we do—grandparents like you and Al have only ten miles away. We're blessed that way, really blessed. If that's the extent of Simon's strangeness, I think you're making a mountain out of a mole hill ... like what you seem to be doing with those mashed potatoes. Don't play with your food, Rachel. Eat it."

"But I haven't told you the rest, Daddy. I reminded him that everybody was having hard times now, with the war and all, when all of a sudden Simon said I didn't know anything at all about *anything* because I'd always lived in the same house in the same town—"

"That's true enough, you haven't had to move like he has," her father pointed out. "I'm about to decide you're irritated because Simon accused you of not knowing anything, Rachel. Is that what this silliness is all about? You haven't said a word about the Nazis, and I thought that's what this conversation was going to be about."

"No, Daddy, no! Just let me finish! I can't remember how it came up, but I said something about hating my initials, and out of the clear blue Simon screamed at me—really screamed, 'Well, what if your initials were S.S., Rachel? S.S. as in Hitler! S.S. as in Nazi! S.S. as in *Schultastaffel*! How would you feel about that? How do you think I feel?'" She stopped to take a breath before she went on. "*Schultastaffel* was a word for the day last month, remember, Daddy? So I knew that's where S.S. came from, but I didn't understand one other thing he was talking about ..."

All three of the members of her audience had stopped eating and were looking at her. Nobody was smiling.

"Simon's initials are not S.S., Rachel," her mother pointed out in a very firm tone. "Simon's last name is Green, and his initials are S.G., not S.S. You just misunderstood what he said. All this war talk on the radio about the German spies, all your listening to 'Captain Midnight.' The newsreels at the picture show. You know how your imagination carries you away. I seem to recall you were absolutely certain John Alan Feester had something to do with the bombing of Pearl Harbor."

"But I wasn't imagining what Simon said, Mama. Simon Green was talking about the S.S.! Do you think maybe he—"

"Everybody talks about the S.S., Rachel. It's in the headlines every day. Simon is a very bright boy. Sylvia tells me he reads the newspaper front to back every day. He's worried about his father. He's worried about our country. That's all there is to it."

"But . . . but . . ." Rachel stammered.

"I think your very vivid imagination combined with your very large vocabulary," her mother said, again giving her father a slicing look, "have made you come to some pretty wild conclusions on no evidence whatsoever. I do not want to hear another word from you about Simon and the Nazis! Do you hear me, Rachel?"

"Yes, Mama," Rachel replied, bowing her head and staring at her half-eaten mashed potatoes and cut-up slice of Spam.

"I have enough to think about without having to worry about you saying something that might upset Sylvia Green, who has become a very close friend of mine. We work together at the Red Cross every day. You drop the subject of Simon and the Nazis entirely, you hear me?"

"I promise. Cross my heart and hope to die," Rachel whispered slashing an X over her heart, "stick red peppers—"

"No! Don't promise that!" her mother interrupted, suddenly bursting into tears. "Don't you ever say that again! I don't want anybody promising to *die*! There's too much real dying going on in the world to make light of death with a silly little poem!"

"Your mother's right, Rachel," Mr. Dalton added,

getting up to pat his wife's shoulder. "This war's got us all on edge, knocked us all off center, kids and grownups, too. Simon's father's off fighting somewhere. We need to give his family our support, not worry them with silly questions. We've all got to stick together and tough it out. For The Duration, you know."

"Yes, Daddy, I know," she sighed. "I know, but I don't understand."

"Nobody does, Red," Al told her, shaking his head. "Nobody understands anything. Just like I don't understand why my parents won't sign for me to join the army early so I can help save our country! This war's gonna be over before I get a chance to get over there and fight!"

"Now, Albert, I'm in no mood to start on that again!" Mrs. Dalton swiped her eyes with her napkin and started to rapidly clear the table. "You will finish high school with the rest of your class next spring, and that's that! Rachel, it's your turn to dry and Al's to wash, so help me pick up the dishes and get on with it! I've got to go back to the Legion Hall and get more bandages wrapped. The blood that's being shed by young men all over Europe every day is the only blood I know of that's bad, and those boys need our bandages to stanch the flow!"

She plopped the dishes she had gathered onto the counter, jerked off her apron, and disappeared through the kitchen door into the living room. Very quickly they heard the front door slamming behind her, but not before they heard her call out, "I'll be waiting in the car, David! Hurry up! And Rachel, tomorrow's laundry day. Separate the whites from the colored in the baskets by the door, and don't forget to empty the pockets!"

"Go easy on your mother, kids," Mr. Dalton said, pushing his chair back to the table. "She's the one that's a little bit crazy these days, not Simon. She's crazy with worry about her brothers. Your grandmother hasn't heard from either of them in over a month. Rachel, do as she asked about Simon, and Al, don't ask your mother to give you up, too. Not until we have to."

He grabbed his hat off the rack and headed for the back door.

"Got to go back to the shop after I drop her at the Legion Hall. This paper shortage has got me scrambling through every old roll I ever saved. Do the dishes, finish your homework, sort the laundry, and get to bed. Don't know how late your mother will be, but I'll wait to bring her home. Gas'll be rationed by fall, so might as well start saving it now. You two can hold down the fort. You're old enough to be on your own."

"Old enough to do everything but join the army!" Al grumbled as he turned on the hot water and began to fill the sink, but his father made no reply before he closed the back door behind him.

"Come on, Red, let's finish up so we can get on with the really important things in life ... homework! Can't believe they think I'm gonna worry about algebra when other guys my age are worrying about having enough bullets in their guns or bombs in their planes!"

Rachel picked up her towel and began to dry. "Al, can I just tell you one more thing about Simon and the Nazis? I mean, I know I promised Mama ... but there's one more thing I just got to tell somebody or I'll pop."

"One more thing, Red," he sighed. "But this is the *very* last time you can bring up Simon and the Nazis. You heard what Mom said."

"Well, I didn't get to tell the strangest thing Simon said." She lowered her voice to a whisper in case there were any spies or traitors nearby. "The strangest thing of all. About his initials. Simon Green told me if the *hungry* people ever found him, his initials would be S.S. again."

"The hungry people?" Al repeated slowly as he pulled the plug to let the water out of the sink. "Who was he taking about? What hungry people?"

"That's just it! I don't know! We hadn't said anything about food!" She stopped wiping and went over to take a bite of her bread pudding. "Then, right before he ran off," she added, wiping her mouth on the towel, "he grabbed me by the shoulders real hard like this!" She took Al's shoulders in both hands and squeezed. "And he screamed, right in my face, Al, he really screamed, '*The* mother and *the* father are the only parents I ever had! I'm Simon Green, their only son! I'm not acting! Don't you ever say the word adopted to me again!' That's what he said! His exact words! I'm positive about that, Al! Absolutely positive!"

"Adopted?" Al frowned as he picked up another towel and began to help her dry. "Now you lost me completely! Had you asked him something about him being adopted, Red? Had you ... well, you know how sometimes your mouth gets away from you. Had you asked something you shouldn't have? Adoption's a very private matter. Not something you pry into."

"That's just it, Al. We weren't talking about adoption. Not then, anyway. At least I didn't think we were. I thought we were talking about John Alan moving away. And why would Simon say 'the' parents instead of 'my' parents? I know I'm right about that, too. He screamed, '*The* mother and *the* father are the only parents I ever had!' If a person is adopted, he has two sets of parents, doesn't he? Why'd he say 'the' instead of 'my'? And why'd he say, 'I'm not acting'?"

"Got no idea, Rach. No idea at all. But like Mom told you, it's better to keep your nose out of other people's private business, so that's what you'd better do." He patted her head. "Well, that's the last of the dishes, so I'm hitting the books. Don't forget to sort those clothes. And turn off the lights in here when you're through. 'When not in use, turn off the juice!'" he laughed, repeating their grandfather's favorite jingle as the swinging doors snapped shut behind him.

Rachel sighed as she dumped the contents of both laundry baskets on the floor. She arranged one basket on the linoleum at the north end of the kitchen and the other at the south end and balled each item up before she shot it into its proper basket. If it went in cleanly, nothing hanging on the sides, her basket won both the game *and* the state championship!

When she picked up her red shorts, she noticed a

bulge in the pocket and remembered Simon's handkerchief. As she pulled it out, she saw a monogram on the corner, a monogram so small she had to move under the bright light over the sink to read it. She smoothed the wrinkled corner flat with her thumbs and sucked in her breath as the tiny red "S.S." appeared.

"S.S.!" she exclaimed. "Simon Green has a handkerchief with the initials S.S. on it!"

And there was nobody in the world she could tell.

CHAPTER 12
The Best of Times

"If you don't pick that face up off the floor, somebody's going to step on it," his mother teased when Simon shuffled his way to the breakfast table and slumped in his chair. He hadn't slept very well because he'd had bad dreams all night, but he couldn't remember what they were about.

He picked up the newspaper and couldn't stop himself from reading the headline about the German saboteurs before he quickly flipped to the sports page. "TRIBUNAL ENDS; VERDICT SOON," the headline read. The sooner the better! But right now all he wanted to think about was baseball. He would *not* let his mind go back down into that basement again. He planned to memorize the box scores from every single baseball game played that week. That would keep his mind away from thoughts of basements and trunks and postcards from hungry people.

"Mr. Schwartz says he's going to send a search party out looking for you," Sylvia chattered, ignoring his sullen mood. "When I was in his shop yesterday, he said he hasn't seen you in three whole days! He needs you to come by this morning. Early. As soon as you finish eating, in fact. It sounded very important. A matter of national security!" She hummed as she poured his orange juice and milk, spooned oatmeal into his bowl, and dropped a piece of buttered toast onto his plate.

"What's he want?" Simon muttered, running his finger down the page until he found the Yanks' and the Tigers' box scores. The Yankees were still in the race, but the Tigers didn't have a chance for the pennant, not with Greenberg off in the army.

Hank Greenberg was Simon's favorite player, even if he was a Tiger instead of a Yankee. Hank, the first Jew to make Most Valuable Player in either league, was Mr. Schwartz's favorite, too. Maybe that was what he wanted to talk about, Hank Greenberg and the Tigers. A week never went by without Mr. Schwartz asking Simon to describe the big game he had been to with his father, the game where every-body thought Greenberg would break Babe Ruth's home run record. They both knew how the story ended, that Hank would get walked every time, but Mr. Schwartz still liked to hear about it from an eye-witness.

"Well," his mother said, drawing the word out as much as possible, "I guess I'll have to tell you this much ... He's got a surprise for you, Mr. Schwartz does. A really grand surprise! The world is full of grand surprises!" She mussed his hair before she sat down.

"Did ... did he read something in the paper about Dad's ship? Something good?" Simon cried, jumping up from the table and knocking his chair over backwards in the process.

"Oh, no, sweet Simon," she said, biting her lip. "They don't put things like that in the paper. You know that. Not after Pearl Harbor. That's not why I'm happy. But you're *really* going to like what Mr. Schwartz has for you. I can guarantee it! Now, that being said, eat your breakfast slowly, chew every bite ten times, and—"

But Simon, who was already out of his seat, had decided breakfast could wait. Mr. Schwartz had a grand surprise! He could use a grand surprise to take his mind off his troubles. He charged out the back door, leaving his upended chair in the middle of the floor and the paper on the table.

"Don't throw that paper out," he called over his shoulder. John Alan Feester might not be keeping close track of those eight German saboteurs, but Simon Green sure was.

Mr. Schwartz was sweeping the floor of his butcher shop when Simon bolted in through the screen door, almost upending the big yellow and white salt blocks stacked in a pyramid in front of the counter.

"Hey, there, Master Green! Don't knock my blocks off!" Mr. Schwartz laughed. "May be rationing salt before this war's over."

"Who buys those things anyway?" Simon asked, licking his finger and swiping it across the top of each block. "And does the white one taste different from the yellow one? To the animals, I mean. Tastes the same to me."

"Don't know the answer to that, Simon. Guess you'd have to ask a cow or deer. They're the ones that lick 'em. Speaking of deer, was that you I saw bounding down the street like Bambi the day John Alan left town?" He leaned on his broom and broke into a grin. "That forest fire didn't get Bambi, and it sure wouldn't a caught you! Maybe a boy who can run like a deer doesn't need a bicycle. What do you think?"

"A bicycle?" Simon grumbled. "Nobody's getting a bicycle these days! Haven't you heard? There's a war on! No more bicycles for The Duration!"

"Well, that may not be entirely true," Mr. Schwartz said, clamping his big, hairy hand over Simon's shoulder and guiding him to the back of the shop. "Maybe there's one very special boy left in the world who's about to get a big surprise."

The back room was so dark it took Simon's sun-blinded pupils a while to adjust. But when he could focus again, the first thing he spotted was a bicycle—a very familiar-looking bicycle—parked in the back corner.

John Alan Feester's blue and white Schwinn!

"Loopin' loops, J.A. forgot his bike!" Simon cried, using his favorite Captain Midnight jargon. "Loopin' loops!" he repeated, louder this time. "How'd he make such an awful mistake? How could a guy forget his wheels?"

"He didn't forget it, Simon, he left it here. On purpose."

"On purpose?"

"Mr. Feester, Sr., says there's no safe place to ride a bike where they're going to live. No place to store one even."

"But John Alan could've been real careful ... paid attention ..."

"Los Angeles is one of the busiest cities in the world, Simon, my boy. All those factories, all those defense plants. Mr. Feester says people there drive like they're in the Indianapolis 500, or used to drive the Indy anyway, before it got canceled for The Duration."

"But ... but ... to leave your bike behind ... when they're not making any more!"

"His father says the apartment they'll be living in just has three tiny rooms in it. I read they're renting out broom closets for people to sleep in out there! Guess they must sleep standing up. John Alan's father gave him no choice. Told him to sell it, and he could keep the money himself. But John Alan didn't want to sell it. Wanted to give it away. To you. He asked me to see to it that you got it. I've been trying to run you down for three days."

"You mean ... you mean this is *my* bike now? He *gave* me his bike?"

"Gave it to you free and clear. Wasn't real happy about losing it, of course, but when his father put his foot down, John Alan said he wanted it to go to you. Because you had been such a good friend, his very best friend in fact. That's what he said."

Simon slumped down on a wooden stool and stared at the bicycle.

"But ... but why didn't he give it to me himself? Why'd he leave it here for you to—"

"Said it was easier on him this way, easier for him to just ride it down here and walk out the door instead of having to listen to you say how sorry you were ... try to help him think of ways of keeping it ... all that. I can understand that, can't you?"

"I ... I guess so."

"Said he'd tell you more about it when he wrote you a personal letter. Said I was to be sure and use those exact words ... a *personal* letter."

"A letter? A personal letter? To just me? He's going to write a letter just to me?"

"That's something I didn't quite understand. He asked me if it would be okay for him to write letters to you in care of me. Put my name on the envelope, but the letter inside would be for you. He said he'd let you tell me the why and wherefore of that." He put the broom away and waited for Simon's explanation.

"Well," Simon said, standing up again and scuffing his shoes back and forth on the splintery floor, "you know how nosy Rachel is … well …" He stopped to take a deep breath and then hurried on. "Rachel made John Alan promise to write just one letter to all of us at the same time. To save paper and postage, she said, but it's really because she wants to know every last secret John Alan and I—"

"Say no more!" Mr. Schwartz sighed, shaking his head. "I live with Mrs. Schwartz, remember? 'Penny for your thoughts?' she asks me. 'What you thinking?' she wants to know. Expects me to tell her what I'm thinking before I think it!" He put a hand on each of Simon's shoulders and looked him straight in the eyes. "The less women know, the better, Simon. Take it from me, a man married forty-seven years! I know about women! I'll get your letters to you, and even your own mama won't know … unless you decide to tell her! My lips are zipped!" he intoned, swiping his fingers across his mouth.

"Loose lips sink ships!" Simon responded, striking the finger-to-the-mouth pose displayed on all the navy posters. "That's what we swabbies say!"

"Speaking of swabbies, brings to mind the navy. Any word from your father?"

"Nothing for three weeks and three days. Mom's worn a groove in the sidewalk going to the post office. She and Mr. Kizer are best friends now. She asks about his son, he asks about Dad. I keep telling her it takes a long time for the mail to reach shore, even that fancy new V-mail. Then they have to get it from the shore to us. All the trains and planes are doing military stuff first, so the mail's slow with a capital 'S.' All we know is he's on the USS *Washington* in a body of water somewhere, but nobody knows where. No loose lips on that ship!"

"Well, no use you jawing with an old man when you got a bike ready to split the wind," Mr. Schwartz enthused as he wheeled the bike through the doorway into the shop and maneuvered it between the counters. "Don't want you going out the back door. Too many stickers in that alley. John Alan got B. Arnold Johnson to air up the tires for you. Got to take special care of those tires. Inner tubes are scarce as hen's teeth these days."

Simon held the screen door while the smiling butcher rolled the bike outside and carefully lined up the tires for him.

"On your seat, get set, go!" barked Mr. Schwartz as Simon hopped on his bike and shot off down the sidewalk.

He hadn't gone half a block before he almost collided head on with Agnes Ann Billingsly, who had rounded the corner and was swooping down the sidewalk toward him like a F4F Wildcat heading for a landing.

"Well, look at Simple Simon with wheels!" she screeched as he veered to avoid crashing into her. "One of the original three blind mice! Four Eyes like you should be banned from riding bikes where *normal* people ride!"

Simon didn't respond, didn't even glance her way. He'd learned right away the only intelligent way to respond to Agnes Ann's mean mouth was to ignore it. No kid in Roosevelt School, not even Rachel, got the last word in on Agnes Ann, so Simon never bothered to try.

Who gave a fig what Agnes Ann Billingsly said or thought, anyway? Certainly not Simon Green, with wheels! This bike was enough to make a guy forget a mile-high pile of troubles.

CHAPTER 13
The Worst of Times

Simon pedaled his newly acquired bicycle with its freshly aired tires up and down every sidewalk in town, carefully avoiding all growing-through-the-cracks patches of grass. Stickers loved those spots, and he certainly wasn't going to let a flat tire ruin this day! The last time Rachel got a sticker, she had to wait almost two weeks for a new inner tube because her old one wouldn't hold a patch. He wasn't going to risk that happening to him. He would, however, risk being shot down by enemy aircraft.

Army Air Corps pilot Simon Green adjusted his goggles, hunched over the handlebars of his Curtiss P40 fighter plane, and sighted the enemy in his crosshairs. He squeezed the gun grips with both hands, sending out a barrage of bullets that spelled out "U.S.A." on the silver side of the doomed Japanese Zero. Simon beamed as the Zero spiraled toward the ground, the telltale Rising Suns on its wings and sides setting for the last time!

Simon's grin grew even larger when he stood up to pump the pedals. The wind rippled up and down his body, and when John Alan's face appeared in the air in front of him, bobbing and weaving like a birthday balloon, he wasn't in the least bit surprised. He didn't wish him away this time. John Alan deserved to be the first passenger on Simon Green's maiden voyage!

What a first-class, A-1, crackerjack going-away present John Alan had given him! And in return, Simon had given John Alan ...

Simon threw on his brakes and screeched to a halt.

Nothing! Absolutely nothing—that's what he'd given the person who had rewarded him with his incomparable, magnificent, blue and white Schwinn bicycle! Not a priceless Babe Ruth baseball card, not a leather-bound, limited edition, illustrated copy of *Wind in the Willows*, not even an unopened package of chewing gum, which was almost as rare as the card these days. Simon had been so busy worrying about his own problems and getting mad and stomping ants, he hadn't even bothered to tell his best friend good-bye!

He climbed back on the bike and started pumping again, this time going only fast enough to keep from falling over. He had some big-time explaining to do to John Alan Feester. He'd do it, too, in writing, just as soon as J.A. got a mailing address. He'd write him a long letter of apology as well as a thank you. Furthermore, he'd keep looking and looking until he found that rare and wonderful Babe Ruth baseball card; then he'd slip that card in the middle of that leather-bound, limited edition of *Wind in the Willows* to create the most surprising and amazing bookmark of all time! It didn't matter that *Wind in the Willows* was a little kid's book. John Alan liked it, and he didn't have his copy anymore. He'd wrap the stupendous gift up in fancy paper, pack it in a sturdy box, and ship it off to California parcel post.

He picked up speed and began to warble "California, Here I Come!" as best he could with the wind bouncing the words around in his mouth as soon as they formed. What a day!

But ... he skidded to a stop once more. Retrieving that book meant he would have to go back down in that basement again, back down into that black hole filled with all those smells and memories. The black hole that held the trunk and its tin box with the hungry people inside.

He had promised himself not to think about that postcard anymore. He was an actor, and he was going to *act* like there was no postcard. He was going to act like there were no hungry people.

He pedaled harder. He needed to be somebody else, somebody who wasn't starting to feel like he wanted to throw up, somebody who wasn't starting to feel like he wanted to hit somebody, somebody who wasn't starting to feel like he was about to remember how to cry.

He headed for the grand and glorious stage in Daddy Warbucks'. He'd rest from his ride in the comfort of the trees and then perform a late-morning, one-man movie for his ever-appreciative horse apple audience. Ever since he saw *Snow White and the Seven Dwarfs* when he was eight, acting out entire movies was his favorite pastime. The more characters the better.

As he turned the corner that led to the trees, an enormous black dog charged out from behind a nearby hedge. Simon's heart skipped a beat when he recognized Spike, Jake Billingsly's meanest mongrel. Spike gave a deep-throated growl and lunged straight for Simon's foot.

In one swift move, Simon pushed down hard on the higher pedal, plopped his bottom back onto the seat, and threw both legs up in the air just below the handlebars. The maneuver bought a split second reprieve, a split second in which a squirrel racing down one of the horse apple trees diverted the dimwitted dog's attention. By the time Simon jerked his head around to see what had happened, Spike was streaking down the street in the other direction in hot pursuit of his bushy-tailed quarry.

"Hey, Spike!" Simon shouted at the dog's disappearing tail. "You scared the Beelzebub out of me! But you gave me a great idea, too! It's the dog days of August, right? Come one, come all! Follow me to Warbucks' Hall! Now showing, *The Hound of the Baskervilles,* starring Basil Rathbone as Sherlock Holmes and Spike Billingsly as the hound!"

Simon and his father had seen *The Hound of the Baskervilles* so many times he could repeat the dialogue almost word for word. He could act out it out from start to finish, play every part including the hound. If nobody came along to interrupt, he could make his performance last until dinnertime!

He skidded his bike to a stop next to the southernmost tree and leaped to the ground. After he lowered the kickstand, he began to drum his fingers on the seat while he conjured up the opening scene from Sir Arthur Conan Doyle's mysterious tale of murder and intrigue.

Simon Sherlock Holmes adjusted his imaginary plaid cape, clutched the curved bowl of his meerschaum pipe in his left hand, and pretended to peer through a magnifying glass with his right.

"Elementary, my dear Watson, elementary!" he proclaimed.

Simon knew Sherlock Holmes didn't use a giant magnifying glass. He didn't repeatedly reproach his doctor friend with, "Elementary, my dear Watson," either. But, since most people seemed to think Holmes actually did those things, Simon, both producer and director as well as actor, decided to weave them into his opening scene.

The world's most famous private detective began to patrol the mansion's dirt floor, carefully inspecting the thick layer of dust that lay there with his magnifying glass. He was almost to the middle of the diamond-shaped floor when he saw it.

A Nazi swastika.

Drawn in the brown-shirt colored dust, on the floor of Daddy Warbucks' tree-guarded mansion, was a Nazi swastika the size of a wagon wheel.

Simon closed his eyes as tight as he could, took a deep breath, and waited for the swastika to disappear. His imagination was playing tricks on him. That's what it was, his imagination! He *thought* he'd left all the troubles that were haunting him outside the trees—the German saboteurs, the S.S. with their shiny black jackboots—but evidently one of them had slipped through and etched a swastika on the floor. He'd wait a full minute, count from one to one hundred, and then, when he opened his eyes again, the swastika would be gone.

He waited. And counted. And opened his eyes.

The swastika was still there.

Simon cautiously approached the closest tip, being careful not to let even the toe of his shoe touch it. He had to get a closer look. Since he had arrived in America five years ago, the only swastikas he had seen were in newsreels at the movie theaters, enormous monsters smeared in what he knew was blood red paint even though the film was black and white. They appeared on walls and buildings, first all over Germany, then across all of Europe.

But this swastika, this dirty, dust-etched symbol of Hitler's horrible power, had been drawn this very day, drawn on his stage in Daddy Warbucks' mansion, the one spot on earth Simon Singer ... No, not

Simon *Singer*! ... Simon *Green* had thought was safe. Drawn to remind both of them that no place on earth was safe, no place at all.

He had to get away immediately, as far away as possible.

He was about to turn and run for his bicycle when he felt the hand on this shoulder. The hand of someone who had slipped up behind him so quietly, so stealthily, he had not heard him coming. The Nazis had found him at last!

Simon Green fell to his knees, covered his face with his hands, and allowed the dam that held back five years of tears to burst.

CHAPTER 14
Rachel to the Rescue

"Simon, why don't you give me your glasses?" he heard Rachel whisper after several minutes—or maybe it was hours—had passed. The moment he felt the hand on his shoulder, time began to telescope in such a way he couldn't tell the minutes from the hours.

"Please let me have your glasses," she pleaded, a little louder this time.

"Tears mess up your lenses something awful. I know that for a fact! I cry when we salute the flag, remember? I can clean your glasses for you. Shine 'em up real good! Please, let me do *something* to help you, Simon. Okay?"

Without lifting his head or uncurling his body,

Simon slipped off his glasses, folded in the ear-pieces, and handed them to her.

But he didn't stop crying.

Rachel checked to be sure no one was watching before she pulled his handkerchief out of her pocket. She had washed it out by hand in the locked bathroom and dried it on a hanger in the back of her dark closet. Now she used it to carefully polish Simon's lenses while she shifted her eyes between the tiny red "S.S." in the corner and the Nazi swastika in the dust.

"Rachel?" he hiccupped at last. "Have you ... did you ... did you see it?"

"I saw it, Simon. I can see it right now."

"Don't touch it!" he warned, still not looking up. "Don't even go near it! It might ... it could ..."

"Oh, Simon, I'm not afraid of a stupid Nazi swastika!" she declared loudly. Clutching his glasses in one hand and his handkerchief in the other, Rachel Elizabeth Dalton stomped over to the swastika and began kicking the dust in all directions. "Glad I got on shoes! I'm gonna obliterate this thing!" She quickly pressed the handkerchief to her palm with her thumb, so she could wave the four fingers triumphantly in the air. "Word for the day last Thursday. 'Obliterate: to erase or completely blot out; to destroy entirely.' Help me, Simon! We're going to obliterate this awful thing!"

Simon's head snapped up, and his puffy eyes widened when he realized what she was doing.

"But Rachel! What if ... what if ... the Nazis ... what if the S.S. ... "

"We'll obliterate them, too, that's what we'll do! Captain Midnight said they might come to America, and sure enough, they did! Those rotten German saboteurs! But we caught them, didn't we? The FBI caught them right away! We'll catch the next ones, too! If there *are* any next ones!"

"But Rachel, you don't understand! I'm the one ... I came ... It's *me* they're after!"

Rachel stopped stomping and stared at him. She'd promised her mother not to ask Simon any more questions, not to pry into his private life. No, wait a minute! She hadn't promised! When she started to say, 'Cross my heart, hope to die ...' her mother yelled at her not to say it, not to wish herself dead. So she hadn't promised!

Besides, she wasn't prying. She was helping. Simon had loaned her his handkerchief, and she had to give it back. She plopped down on her knees in front of him and held out his glasses in one hand and his handkerchief in the other with the red initials pinched between her thumb and forefinger so they could not be seen.

"You ... you said you wanted your handkerchief back, Simon. It ... it looks really old. Like it's been in your family for a very long time."

Simon eyed the cream-colored cloth with the hidden "S.S." on the corner, but he reached for his glasses first. Keeping his eyes on Rachel, he took a long time unfolding them and positioning them on his nose and ears before he grabbed the handkerchief without looking at it. He shoved it in his pocket and took a very deep breath.

Rachel wanted very badly to know about those initials. Simon wondered what he should say. If he told her about the initials, she'd want to know a whole lot more. John Alan called Rachel a professional question asker. Simon had promised his father to never talk about his past, never tell anything, but his father had left him to join the navy, left him just like all the others. He might even be dead by now.

His mother and father, his Polish grandmother and Hannah, they might all be dead, too. Dead or in concentration camps. Only he and his mother were left, and if the Nazis with their terrible swastika found them ... That postcard had found him. The hungry people knew where he was!

He needed help. He was afraid of the Nazis, but Rachel wasn't afraid of anything, not of that swastika or the Nazis or anything else. She'd marched right over and obliterated that Nazi swastika!

Maybe, he thought, someone else could tell Rachel his story. Maybe someone who knew all the lines could act it out for him. That wouldn't be breaking his promise to his father. Not if someone who wasn't Simon Green did all the talking.

Simon jumped up, grabbed Rachel's hands, and pulled her to her feet. He motioned her to the large exposed roots she and John Alan called their box seats. He smiled as she pretended to tuck the long skirt of a theater gown under her before she sat down on the hard, dusty ground.

Simon marched over to where the swastika had been and took Rachel's courage as his own. He brushed the floor with his feet until the ground was smooth and flat again, and then he stood in the middle of the stage and bowed as if he were in the spotlight.

"My name ... my name is Simon Singer," he began in a voice that somehow sounded much younger than his own, "and I am a German Jew."

Rachel, who had been casually leaning back against the tree holding a stick next to her eyes like the handle on opera glasses, dropped the stick, sat up very straight, and sucked in her breath.

"At the age of five years, three hundred fifty-five days," Simon continued in a slow and measured tone, "I was put on the SS *New York* bound for the United States of America. Behind me, in Stuttgart, Germany, I left my dear mother, my beloved sister, Hannah, and ..." He paused to iron all the hurt out of the next words, "... And my father, whose decision it was to send me away."

Simon Green often chose to become people who had endured great agony because he could experience their triumphs without feeling their pain. But when Simon Green became Simon Singer once more, Simon Singer's pain became his own.

CHAPTER 15
The Truth at Last

Rachel didn't applaud as she usually did when Simon ended a performance. Her hands were too busy wiping away her tears. She shook her head back and forth so many times, Simon finally had to go over and put a hand on either side of her face to stop the motion. He left one hand on her cheek while he reached in his pocket, pulled out his handkerchief, and wiped her cheeks with it.

"Now you understand. About those initials, I mean."

She nodded her head, but she didn't reply. For the first time since Simon Green had met her, Rachel Elizabeth Dalton was speechless.

"It's ... it's just another war story, Rachel," he

144

sighed after several minutes of silence had passed. "We see war movies at the picture show every week now, don't we? It's just that my particular story happens to be true. Most of those at the picture show aren't."

"I knew that, Simon. The minute you started talking, I knew it was true. I knew you weren't acting." She felt the blood rush to her cheeks where he had touched them. "Nobody could make up that story. Not even you! To think that I have a friend that . . . I know a person . . . I actually know a person who . . . I know you, Simon Singer!"

"I . . . I had to tell somebody, Rachel . . . I . . . had to," he stuttered. "When I saw that swastika, I just had to. I'm glad it was you. I feel better now. I didn't think I would, but I do." He turned to stare across the vacant playground. "All of that happened a long time ago," he sighed.

"No wonder you called me a sniveling baby! Complaining about my stupid initials! Carrying on about Paul moving to California. When you lost your home, your family . . . And then, you find that postcard—"

"I never called you a sniveling baby, Rachel," he interrupted. The postcard from those hungry people was not something he wanted to discuss anymore.

Not today, anyway. "You would have slapped me up the side of the head if I called you a sniveling baby," he teased.

"You thought it, though! And I don't blame you! Don't blame you a bit! I *am* a sniveling baby! I can't imagine how you put up with—"

"Loose lips sink ships," Simon hissed as he tapped her mouth with one finger before he sprinted over to his bike and began to inspect the back tire. "We're about to get blitzed!" he muttered as he tilted his bike to the ground and began to run his fingers over the treads as if he were searching for a sticker.

"Well, well, well, if it isn't a meeting of the Blind as a Bat Club!" Agnes Ann Billingsly brayed as she skidded to a halt next to Rachel's bike. "Eight eyes instead of four! How come you bats are down here instead of hanging upside down in the trees?"

Simon didn't look up, so Rachel bit her tongue and sauntered over to supervise his sticker search.

"Isn't that John Alan Feester's fancy Schwinn you got there? What'd ja do, swipe it off the moving van?"

"Jump on your broom and fly home, Agnes Ann!" Rachel snipped. "Spike's looking for a bone to chew, and I volunteered your leg!"

Agnes Ann narrowed her eyes at Rachel.

"What time we supposed to be at school Monday,

Miss My-daddy-owns-the-newspaper-know-it-all? Can't believe we're startin' back the eighth of August! My old man says it's 'cause of the war, and all those crummy farmers' kids we got in our school! Cotton pickers, that's all they are!"

"My daddy says farmers are the bravest people ever born 'cause they have to battle Mother Nature!" Rachel retorted. "Everybody in town knows about *your* daddy. He's nothing but an un-American, un-patriotic black marketeer, that's what your daddy is!"

The minute she spat out the words and saw Agnes Ann's face fall, Rachel regretted her own meanness, but her words had been tossed in the air, and there was no way to grab them back.

"You leave my daddy out of this, Red," Agnes Ann said, shaking her fist at both of them. "You still haven't answered my school question. Maybe you don't know about school time, huh?"

"Same as last year, nine to four," Rachel sighed, regret smoothing the edge off her tone. "War Time, of course. We got to start early August so we can let out the whole month of September instead of half like most years. So many farmers in the military now, everybody who can drag a sack's gonna be picking cotton! How about you, Agnes Ann? You gettin' a cotton picking sack?"

147

"Me? Pick cotton? That red hair's cooked your brain! I'm of a delicate nature! Get sick easy! Mostly I'm sick of this war! No candy, no ice cream, no sugar, no gum, no—"

"You're really having to suffer, aren't you, Agnes Ann?" Rachel screamed. "Well, let me tell you about somebody who—"

"Well, Rachel, that does it!" Simon yelled before she could finish. "Tire's all fixed and ready to roll. Excuse us, Agnes Ann, Captain Midnight just called on the walkie-talkie. Got a secret mission for Rachel and me, so we gotta go!" He gave Rachel a thumbs-up as he jerked his bike into the upright position and jumped on.

"Loopin' loops! Can't keep the Captain waiting!" Rachel cried as she, too, mounted her bike and positioned her feet on the pedals.

"Watch out for spies and traitors! Captain Midnight says they're all around us!" Simon warned as they shot off down the sidewalk, leaving Agnes Ann standing in the middle of Daddy Warbucks' mansion looking as if she had a lot more she wanted to say.

CHAPTER 16
Sneaking Suspicions

"Simon, you got to explain something to me," Rachel said between sips of water while he held the drinking fountain handle down for her. They'd ridden their bikes around town for quite some time before they ended up in the city park. Rachel, who was trying to fit the facts of Simon's two lives together like the pieces of a complicated jigsaw puzzle, hadn't said a word the whole time.

"What I don't understand," she went on, holding the handle while he took his turn, "is why you think whoever drew that swastika was a Nazi and that he did it because of you. You're just a kid."

"But I'm a Jew, Rachel! It's Jews they're after!"

"But Simon, Mr. Schwartz is a Jew, too! How come they didn't draw swastikas on his store? Everybody knows he's Jewish. Nobody knows about you. Besides, even though I wouldn't be at all surprised if we had some spies around here—Captain Midnight says we might—I can't believe a Nazi would come all the way to Apache, Oklahoma, looking for a Jewish kid who left Germany five years ago. That's crazy!"

"I . . . I hadn't thought about it that way," Simon admitted as he strolled over to a big oak tree and flopped down on his belly in the grass it shaded. "I hadn't thought about it logically. When you've been afraid for a long time, afraid like we were, even when things change, when your life gets really good again . . . those days, those bad times are still there . . . in the back of your head somewhere . . ." He stopped to ruffle his fingers through the grass as if the words he was looking for might be hidden in the blades.

"The first swastika I ever saw, the one on my father's store, was still wet, Rachel. It was still dripping jet black and white and blood red paint when I saw it! That memory was branded in my brain so deeply that when I saw the one on the floor of Daddy Warbucks', that dust one turned into the other one, and I just thought . . ." He stopped looking at the grass and looked at her. "I was back in Stuttgart again. I was Simon Singer, looking at that dripping swastika on the wall of my father's store. And I was afraid."

"Can't even imagine that kind of fear, Simon," she admitted. "Not in my worst nightmare ever. I don't think I've ever been *really* afraid of anything, not even when I was a little kid. There just wasn't anything around here to be afraid of."

Then, recalling his ant bed observation, she chanted, "I've lived in the very same house with the very same mother and the very same father and the very same brother all my very same life." She paused to be sure he remembered saying that to her, and when he nodded, she went on. "Fear's never been my word for the day, Simon. I never knew the meaning of it."

"Jews know the meaning of fear."

"But Jews aren't the only people Hitler's after. He wants rid of anybody that's not white and German ... blacks and gypsies, even Jehovah's Witnesses! The Master Race, that's what he says Germans are, the Master Race! That's really, really scary. Master of what, the whole world?"

"Don't know. After seeing that swastika today, there's a whole bunch I don't know. But the more I think about what you just said, you're probably right.

Whoever drew that swastika wasn't after me. He was just trying to stir up trouble. Like the person who threw that brick through the window of Sam Sing's laundry trying to get people riled up against the Japanese. And poor old Mr. Sing is Chinese! Guess that must have scared Mr. Sing as much as that swastika did me. Never did find out who did that, did they?"

"Well, no," Rachel said, looking away quickly so Simon wouldn't see the guilty look on her face. She *did* know about that brick, knew all about who threw it and why, in fact. But she'd crossed her heart never to tell a living soul, and she couldn't break that promise. Not even to Simon Green.

"If that's why he drew the swastika," she hurried on, "to scare people, I mean, it sure worked! It scared you plenty! And now I know what happened to you, I know why! We got to find out who did it so they won't do it again and scare somebody else, but we're going to need help. I vote we draft Kenneth."

"Oh, I don't know, Rachel. I don't think we ought to involve anybody else."

"But, Simon, even Sherlock Holmes had help! Those Baker Street Irregulars found out all sorts of information he'd never been able to find out himself! Kenneth drags that wagon of his all over town. Nobody'd ever suspect him of spying on them!

Besides, he told me all about the swastika being a really sacred Indian symbol till Hitler ruined it. Kenneth's real mad about that! Do you know about that swastika stuff?"

The minute she asked the question, Rachel knew she was in for another performance. Not a surprising performance like Simon's last one, but a performance nevertheless. Since she'd figured out a long time ago that acting made Simon feel better, she just smiled when he stood up and bowed.

"Yes, indeed, eager students, I know all about the history of the Indians and the swastika," he said, rocking back and forth from his heels to his toes. Playing a history professor was his favorite role. "The swastika became the emblem for the Nazi Party on August 7, 1920, at the Salzburg Congress," he declared, adjusting an imaginary monocle on his eye. "Adolph Hitler claims the swastika symbolizes the victory of the German race, the race he calls 'Aryan,' over the rest of the world. When the Indians found this out, they passed laws and ordinances forbidding its use, even the army ..."

"I know the rest," Rachel interrupted, "about the Forty-fifth Division and all. But your incredible store of knowledge caused me to make a decision! We've got to have an Indian who knows about swastikas.

Therefore, we are recruiting Kenneth Stumbling Bear! We also need," she continued poking her finger in her cheek, "to figure out exactly what kind of person would draw that swastika. It would be somebody who was mean, somebody who liked to stir up trouble, somebody like ... like ... Agnes Ann Billingsly! Why didn't I think of her to begin with? She's real mad about the war, she's real mean, and she even came right up to the trees while we were there. Returning to the scene of her crime! Criminals always do that! I read that in detective books. I'm going right back to Daddy Warbucks' and see if she's still there. If she is, I'm going to face her out, tell her we're going to get a warrant out for her arrest!"

"Now, wait a minute, Rachel. We don't have an ounce of proof that Agnes Ann drew that swastika. Let's ..." Simon started to say, but Rachel was already on her bike and pedaling away. He didn't have any choice but to get on his bike and follow.

When they raced up to Daddy Warbucks', Agnes Ann was nowhere to be seen.

But there was something to look at.

Another swastika.

In the dust.

A swastika even larger than the first one.

CHAPTER 17
Justice Swift and Harsh

"Here it comes, the White House press release about the Nazi saboteurs!" Mr. Dalton shouted over the clanking of the presses in the newspaper office the next afternoon. Al, who was in the back room laying out grocery ads, rushed to the Teletype machine and stood next to his father so they could read the words together as they clicked onto the paper, letter by letter.

"Holy Moly, they're already dead!" Al whispered, scanning the sentences as quickly as they appeared. "Started electrocuting them at noon 'according to White House Press Secretary Steve Early.'" He shifted his eyes to the pendulum clock above his father's desk. "It's not even two o'clock, and they're all dead! No, wait! Not all! Six. Six are dead! Other two got their sentences commuted to life for helping the government prove their case."

"That's the justice we needed!" Mr. Dalton cried, slapping his hands together in one loud clap. "It'll do more to protect our country than every plane and ship patrolling both coasts and Canada!" He pulled the sheet of paper from the machine and sat down to read the release a second time. "This is going in the middle of the front page of next week's *Republican,* word for word. Etch it with a black border. Gonna title it 'Justice Swift and Harsh!'" He leaned back in his chair, laced his fingers behind his head, and propped his feet up on the desk. "America's going to sleep better tonight, that's for sure!"

"Those generals sure reached their verdicts in a hurry, didn't they? I don't remember any trial ever ending on a Saturday. I thought courts took the weekends off."

"Wasn't a trial, son, it was a tribunal. Roosevelt insisted on a tribunal because tribunals are fast. He wanted to send those Nazis over there a strong, fast message. Mess with the U.S.A. on our own soil, and you're a walking dead man! Old Hitler's going to have a hard time finding more saboteur henchmen eager to come here, at least for The Duration." He grabbed up the telephone receiver and cranked the handle.

"Clara? Push that fire alarm button, would you?" he barked to the operator. "Nope, no fire, just big news! You tell everybody that grabs up their phone to find out where the fire is to turn on their radios for some mighty good news. There's six less Nazis in the world!"

The alarm rang, the telephones were lifted, and the word was spread.

CHAPTER 18
Schwartz's on Sunday

After he and Rachel found the second swastika, Simon thought it over very carefully and decided he needed to pay Mr. Schwartz a visit. He wasn't sure exactly what he was going to say, but if Rachel was wrong and he was right, if there really were Nazis in their town, Mr. Schwartz needed to know, needed to be warned.

Rachel had been able to brush away his fears, been able to pass her courage on to him temporarily, but after he left her on her driveway, when he was alone in his room in the dark, alone and remembering, all the old fears came back again. He wanted to tell his mother, but that postcard held him back even though he wasn't sure why.

He needed to talk with Mr. Schwartz man to man. So he waited until he was sure Rachel was in Sunday school and then headed for the meat market. Mr. Schwartz always did his bookkeeping on Sunday mornings, so Simon knew he wouldn't be hard to find. He slipped down the alley that led to the back of the shop and rapped softly on the screen door.

"Well, well, if it isn't the King of the Wind! To what do I owe this early morning visit, Simon? Where's your bike? Didn't find yourself a sticker already, did you?"

"It's ... it's not a sticker I found, Mr. Schwartz, it's ... it's Nazi swastikas!" he blurted out even before the screen door had closed behind him. That wasn't what he had planned to say at all, not the way he had meant to begin, but once he caught sight of Mr. Schwartz, the only other Jew in town besides him and his mother, the words jumped out of his mouth before he could stop them.

"Nazi swastikas?" Mr. Schwartz whispered, the color draining from his face as he grabbed Simon's hands in both of his.

"On the playground at the school! In the trees! Two of them! Rachel saw them, too, both of them, so I'm not just imagining them! I'm afraid they've found me, Mr. Schwartz!"

"You? Nazi swastikas? In the trees? What are you saying, Simon? You're not making any sense at all."

"I'm a Jew, Mr. Schwartz. A Jew, like you. I never told you because ... because my father said ... my father told me to never ..."

"Sit down, Simon! Sit down on this bench and calm yourself! I'll pull the shades so no one will bother us." He scurried to the front and had all the shades drawn in a matter of seconds.

"Why don't you start at the very beginning, Simon?" Mr. Schwartz urged. "I would be able to help you better if I knew the whole truth." He reached over and mussed Simon's hair just like his father used to do. Isadore Green loved him very much, loved him enough to understand his need to become Simon Singer one more time. At least for a little while.

"I ... I can tell it better ... tell you all of it if ... if I become the boy I used to be."

"The boy you used to be?" Mr. Schwartz whispered. "And who was this boy, this boy you used to be?"

And for the second time in two days, Simon Green stood and announced in a voice that sounded much younger than his own, "My name is Simon Singer, and I am a German Jew."

CHAPTER 19
Simon's Seder

"Simon, you know the story of Passover, of course?" Mr. Schwartz asked after Simon Singer's performance had ended and a long period of silence had ensued.

"Passover? Yes, I know about Passover. My Polish grandmother ... Simon Singer's Polish grandmother ... had a Seder in our basement when I was four. She explained it all to Hannah and me. My Polish grandmother was the only Orthodox Jew in our family," he whispered. It felt so good to speak of her again, his kind and gentle Polish grandmother. He hadn't known how good—and bad—speaking of her again would feel. "It's hard for me to remember the Seder, but I remember my Polish grandmother."

"Well, my son, the story you have told, the exodus of Simon Singer, The Tale of Simon Green, seems a bit like the Passover story to me. An exodus from your homeland, a life both bitter and sweet, a life washed with oceans of salty tears. Many parallels, I think, dear Simon. Many parallels."

"My mother, my father, my Hannah ... they were Jews, but only by birth, my father always insisted, especially after the Nazis came. We never attended a synagogue, never observed any holidays, but we were Jews. Hitler said so."

"Yes, yes," Mr. Schwartz sighed as if a part of him was hurting, "always the question. To be Jewish. Is it a race? Is it a religion? Is it both? Hitler declared a Jew a Jew if three of the four grandparents were Jews. Others say Jews can only be born of Jewish mothers. How can you be born what you are not? How can you be what you are not born?"

"Sylvia and Isadore Green are Jews, but also only by name." Simon shrugged before he added, "Even though that name was changed from Greenberg to Green." He shook his head and allowed a small smile to form before continuing. "If they'd just left it alone, I'd be kin to Hank and get in all his games for free!" The smile faded. "To be a Jew is to be a tightrope walker, Bernard Singer told me. A tightrope walker who is required to perform without a net."

"You know, of course, why Jews play the violin instead of the piano?" Mr. Schwartz asked, a twinkle momentarily replacing the pain in his eyes.

"Because it's hard to run with a piano on your back," Simon sighed. "All Jews know the answer to that question."

There was another period of silence before Simon spoke again.

"Rachel says I'm crazy to think the Nazis would come all the way across the ocean looking for me. Do you think that, too, Mr. Schwartz?"

"I do not think your fear is irrational, Simon. I will tell you something that I did not tell even Mrs. Schwartz." He lowered his voice. "Back in February, when I first read about the Japanese Americans being loaded into cattle trucks and taken to internment camps, I became frantic to find my naturalization papers. The citizenship ceremony was so long ago, I had misplaced the official papers."

"What did you do?" Simon asked, his hands covering his mouth. Suddenly, he was as afraid for Mr. and Mrs. Schwartz as he was for himself and his mother. If Rachel were wrong, if there really were Nazis here, he had led them right to Mr. Schwartz's door! He realized he never should have come here. What if he'd been followed?

"I went to Anadarko, to the courthouse, and a kind woman who works there wrote to New York, where I took my examination. It took over two months, but she was able to get a copy of my papers. She even called me long distance to tell me the good news."

"But Mr. Schwartz," Simon protested, "you've been in Oklahoma since before statehood! The sign on your shop says 1901. Nobody would ever—"

"They locked up the Japanese, Simon. Some Italians, too, as well as Germans. President Roosevelt himself signed the order! Some of those poor people were third-generation Americans. I'm only first. Jews the world over have targets on their backs. These are crazy times, scary times."

He stopped to shake his head as he ran the fingers of both hands through his steel gray hair. "And now the Nazi swastika has come to the playground of Theodore Roosevelt Elementary School. This is not something to be taken lightly. The appearance of such a symbol raises anti-Semitic feelings. I do not believe a German saboteur is hiding in our town, Simon, but often the threat from within is worse than the one from without. We must look within for the swastika artist."

"Rachel says it was done by a mean person, somebody who wanted to stir up trouble like they show on the newsreels at the picture show all the time. In fact, Rachel's pretty sure she knows who did it. She thinks it's Agnes Ann Billingsly."

"Jake Billingsly's little daughter—drawing Hitler's horrible swastika?" Mr. Schwartz cried. "I can't believe that! I save bones for her dog! I've heard rumors about Jake, Jake and his black market tires. But I can't believe his daughter ... What evidence does Rachel have that Agnes Ann did this terrible thing?"

"The evidence against her is very circumstantial," Simon explained in his lawyer voice. "Purely circumstantial. Rachel and I saw her hanging around the trees on the playground where the swastikas were drawn. Agnes Ann gripes about the war all the time. And she's ... she's not a very nice person, not very *kind*. That's all."

"Agnes Ann, not nice? Not kind? That side of her I have never seen. We talk baseball, Agnes Ann and I. She's also a Greenberg fan." He began to shake his head back and forth. "But I suppose it's possible. Anything is possible. If there is one thing I have learned in seventy-two years of living, it is that anything is possible."

"Agnes Ann Billingsly knows about Hank Greenberg? Loopin' loops! You're right, Mr. Schwartz. If Agnes Ann likes Hank Greenberg, anything's possible!"

"We must think on this trouble a while," Mr. Schwartz added solemnly as he took the pencil from behind his ear and began tapping it on the barrel next to his chair. "We must make a plan before we act. Tell Rachel not to accuse the Billingsly girl until we get some real proof, catch her in the act perhaps. The less noise, the better. Wait a day or two. See if it happens again."

"Maybe now they've electrocuted the saboteurs, the swastika artist will crawl back into his hole," Simon said hopefully. "At least for The Duration."

"That's not long enough, Simon," Mr. Schwartz sighed. "The Duration is not long enough. We must try to stop such things from happening ever again, try to stop one person from putting fear into the heart of another. That is what people who draw swastikas want to do."

A fly, trapped on the screen door, began a loud buzz, so Mr. Schwartz walked over to free it. He flung open the door, banged his hand against the wire, and was closing the door again when something on the ground below the step caught his eye.

Another swastika.

"The wolf has been at my very door, Simon," Mr.

Schwartz sighed, pointing his finger so Simon could see what he was talking about. "Under the shelf which holds the bones for those with hungry dogs!" He pointed to the empty wooden box.

"Agnes Ann Billingsly!" Simon whispered. "You said you saved bones for her dog! She did it while we were talking about her! She heard every word we said!"

"But Simon, I save bones for many people, including your friends Rachel and Kenneth. There are many hungry dogs in this town. I don't keep track of how many dogs I make happy."

"Then maybe it was a Nazi! Maybe I was right to begin with! Maybe there were nine saboteurs! Maybe one of them got away!"

"It is broad daylight. Whoever did this had to walk down the alley in broad daylight on a sunny Sunday morning, Simon. No Nazi, a stranger to our town, could walk that alley unnoticed. People see the alley from their kitchen windows. Only a very tiny child could go by unnoticed. You are letting fear scramble your brains like a breakfast egg. Believe me, Simon, there are no foreign Nazis in our little town."

Simon looked up at Mr. Schwartz and shook his head skeptically.

"Think a moment, Simon. Apache's a small

town, a very small town. The moment a strange car drives down our one main street, every person it passes reads its tag, knows if it is in-state or out, knows the color of the driver's hair."

"You're right. I know it. My head knows it. But it's inside here," he touched his stomach and heart. "My fear lives here!"

"How I wish I could sweep it away for you," Mr. Schwartz said as he picked up his broom and began to dust the swastika away, "but that is something only you can do, Simon. Only you." He paused for a moment before he added, "School starts tomorrow, doesn't it? That should make watching the Billingsly girl a little easier, shouldn't it?"

"Sure. For almost half of the day she'll be in somebody's sight, mostly that of Miss Sadie Oxley. When they promoted us to sixth grade last year, they promoted Miss Oxley, too. You know about that?"

"Yes, I heard. My meat market is a confessional, you know. All the troubles they have, the customers bring to my counter. The smallness of my shop, the fact that often there are only two of us in here, invites such confidences, I think. Miss Sadie is a hard taskmaster, I understand. *Odious* Oxley, she is called by some, I believe." He stopped sweeping and peered at Simon over the top of his glasses. "I hope you are not one of the rude children who call her by that name, Simon. It is disrespectful to speak of one's teacher in that manner."

"Oh, well," Simon said, scuffing the floor and avoiding eye contact, "that was the nickname Rachel gave her last year. Before she found out Miss Oxley listens to 'Captain Midnight' and drinks Ovaltine! After she found that out, and then when Miss Oxley volunteered to teach B. Arnold Johnson how to read, Rachel decided 'odious' didn't fit anymore. So now she calls her 'Sadie, Sadie, old maid lady.' But not where Miss Oxley can hear her."

"*Oye, ve*! Children," Mr. Schwartz lamented as he hung his broom back on its hook just outside the back door. "Remember, Simon, teachers, too, must take the bitter with the sweet! Always be the sweet, Simon. Always be Miss Oxley's sweet."

Mr. Schwartz slowly lowered himself onto the back step, his knees cracking so loudly in protest that Simon found himself rubbing his hands up and down his own legs in sympathy. The old man patted the worn wooden board next to him, inviting Simon to join him on the still shaded step.

"Such quiet knees you have, my Simon," Mr. Schwartz said with a chuckle. "I should have such quiet knees! Maybe I should have been a first baseman instead of a catcher, you think? Maybe I should have been Hank Greenberg?"

"You played catcher? You never told me that! All the time we've talked baseball, you never told me that. You never told me Agnes Ann was a fan of Hank's either. Agnes Ann ... a Greenberg fan!" He shook his head slowly back and forth. "I could make a riddle out of that!"

"We all have our secrets, Simon. Some of them are big, some of them are small, but we all have secrets." Mr. Schwartz picked up a small rock, rubbed it into an imaginary glove, and returned it to an imaginary pitcher. "Sometimes, Simon," he lowered his voice to the softest of whispers, "sometimes, when I listen to Hank play on the radio, I pretend that I am the great Greenberg!"

He turned to look at Simon, who was shaking his head back and forth and smiling more than he had smiled in a very long time.

"You must not tell Mrs. Schwartz, of course," Mr. Schwartz went on, poking Simon in the ribs with one finger. "She sometimes catches me being Hank Greenberg at the bat, and she says to me, 'Leo, what are you thinking? What brings that smile to your face?' You think I'm going to tell her I just knocked four home runs in one game? Better I should say I am dreaming of Miss Sadie Oxley! *That* she would think was a joke. Hank Greenberg knocking home runs—she would say I was *meshuga!*"

"*Meshuga,*" Simon repeated softly. Crazy. *Meshuga* means crazy. It had been such a long time since he'd heard that favorite word of his Polish grandmother.

The morning sun warmed the weed-filled alley during the happy silence that followed Mr. Schwartz's confession. A slight breeze lifted and dropped the leaves of the bushes that framed the back door to the shop.

"Now that I know your story, now that I know of your life as Simon Singer, I understand your fears, Simon Green. But I also know fears can be overcome. If, for the present time, acting is the only way you can overcome these fears, then act, act! Shakespeare says we are all actors! I studied a little Shakespeare long ago," Mr. Schwartz confided, leaning back and looking at the sky. "'This above all: to thine own self be true.' Nine of the strongest words ever strung together." He turned to look straight into Simon's eyes.

"When peace comes to the world again, it will also come to your heart and soul, Simon. I am as sure of that as I am that the sun will come up tomorrow.

The time will come when you will not be required to act anymore because you will have turned into the person you wish to be. 'To thine own self be true.'"

Mr. Schwartz put his arm around Simon's shoulder, and for the first time since Simon Singer slipped out of his life, Simon Green did not feel as if his heart were beating in two separate chambers.

CHAPTER 20
King of the Jews

"I got a riddle nobody in the whole sixth grade can solve!" Agnes Ann Billingsly announced to the kids who were milling around the playground, waiting for the bell to ring the next morning. Since their classroom was going to be in the old metal bus barn again, hot in the summer, freezing in the winter, nobody was in the mood for riddles.

"Riddles are for fifth graders," Rachel shot back. "Grow up!" But she didn't take her eyes off Agnes Ann in her wrinkled red Dale Evans cowgirl skirt with its matching vest and boots. Rachel started to point out that sixth-grade girls, mature sixth-grade girls anyway, no longer wanted to grow up to be Dale

Evans either. But then she remembered the hurt on Agnes Ann's face when she called her father a black marketeer, so she bit her tongue and kept quiet.

Agnes Ann charged over and got nose to nose with Rachel before she began chanting:

"Nebuchadnezzar, King of the Jews,
got up one morning to tie his shoes!
Can you spell that with four letters?"

King of the Jews? Was that what she just said? King of the Jews? Rachel whipped around to make eye contact with Simon. Had he heard what Agnes Ann said? What more proof did he need? Agnes Ann Billingsly was the swastika artist! Her stupid riddle proved it! Nobody else went around talking about Jewish kings!

Simon shook his head and stared at the ground as he strolled away toward the trees, so Rachel bit her tongue even harder and looked down, too. Was he looking for another swastika? She tried to get his attention, but he was too busy looking at the ground to notice.

Agnes Ann turned to the group again and repeated, louder this time:

"Nebuchadnezzar, King of the Jews,
got up one morning to tie his shoes!
Can you spell that with four letters?"

Silence again.

"Isn't there even *one* smart person in this stupid class?" she jeered. "One person who knows something about the Bible? Nebuchadnezzar's a Bible name! He was a king, a Jew king!"

"T-h-a-t," Simon spelled in a whisper to Rachel, who had turned on her heel and was following him to Daddy Warbucks' as she scanned the streets looking for Paul, who was overdue in returning from California.

Rachel stopped looking to reply, "What'd you say?"

"T-h-a-t," Simon repeated. "The answer to Agnes Ann's riddle. It's that ... t-h-a-t. Her riddle ended, 'Can you spell *that* with four letters?' But she's not much of a Bible scholar. Nebuchadnezzar wasn't King of the Jews. The Jews didn't like them at all. I say 'them' because there were at least four different kings named Nebuchadnezzar. Most of them were really mean, especially to the Jews."

"Is there anything you don't know, Simon?" Rachel sighed, sitting down next to him on one of the root benches. "Anything in the whole wide world you can't give a lecture on? If you're so smart, why don't you know who's drawing those swastikas? Don't you think it's strange our number-one suspect is asking a riddle about the King of the Jews? People who draw swastikas don't like Jews!"

Simon started to tell her he knew for a fact that Agnes Ann liked at least one Jew, Hank Greenberg, but he stopped himself. If he told her that much, she'd want to know how he knew something so personal about Agnes Ann. Then she'd want to know why he went to Mr. Schwartz's without her.

"I have as much trouble keeping up with your logic as I do keeping up with Gus Stumbling Bear, Rachel," Simon told her, smacking her arm like John Alan used to smack his, but not nearly as hard. "I spent two whole hours helping Kenneth look for that kid Saturday. We were almost glad when he turned up with chickenpox, but I'm not sure even chickenpox will keep Gus home. I did put the search time to good use, though. I recruited Kenneth to help us find the guy who's drawing the swastikas."

"Or *girl*! I told you Kenneth'd be great. Indians know all there is to know about tracking! Glad I had the chickenpox already. Mama says a whole slew of kids have them. She's been short of bandage folders for a week. Kenneth and Paul and I all got chickenpox at the same time when we were in first grade. Paul and I had everything at the same time." She looked up and down the street again.

"That's itchy stuff anytime, but when it's this hot, it must be worse! I had them in the winter, and I had Zinziberi to help me scratch the hard-to-reach places. Irish setters are very smart, you know. You can teach them to do anything!" Simon sighed, as he always did when he thought about the dog he had to leave behind in Pennsylvania.

"You miss that dog something awful, don't you, Simon? What'd you say that funny name of hers means?"

"Roots of the ginger plant. I was up to the Z's in my encyclopedia when my dad brought her home. I was just seven, so lots of the words were too hard for me to read, but the pictures were great! Some of them were even in color! My father promised that when I'd studied every picture on every page in the whole set from front to back, he'd get a smart dog to teach me how to read all those big words. He had ... has ... a goofy sense of humor, my dad."

"I know you miss him most of all. Lots more than I miss Paul even." She looked up and down the street again so she wouldn't have to look at him. "I ... I think you got more to miss than anybody I ever knew in my whole life, Simon. I don't see how you stand it. I go to sleep every night thinking about what's happened to you, all those people who just disappeared from your life at the same time. I try to imagine what that would feel like, but I can't. I can't at all." She scooted over to pat him on the shoulder, and then quickly scooted back.

"You get used to it. Kind of like when you pull a tooth. Remember how at first your tongue looks for it all the time, pokes down in that hole where the tooth used to be even when you try to make it not do that anymore? But, after a while, you finally get used to it, and your tongue stops looking. It's ... it's a little bit like that anyway. Your heart can only hurt so long, then it kind of gets numb."

Rachel couldn't think of a reply to that, so she was relieved when she saw Agnes Ann sneaking around the corner of the building.

"Hey, our prime suspect just disappeared!" she whispered. "Got to see where's she going! You wait here for Kenneth!"

Simon stood up and began to scuff his new shoes back and forth on the spot where the swastika had been, the spot where he had become Simon Singer for Rachel. In spite of Mr. Schwartz's assurances, his life still seemed as tangled as his grandmother's spools of thread on the night the Gestapo came for her. As they stomped out the door, one of the Nazis had grabbed the sewing box out of her arms and flung it across the room. Simon and Hannah spent the rest of the night trying to find and untangle the many spools of thread and to understand why their grandmother would have chosen to take her sewing box instead of her suitcase.

"They have ripped our lives beyond mending," she had sobbed as the Nazis dragged her out the door. "They have ripped our hearts open forever!"

He needed to tell his mother that story. He had never been allowed to tell his stories to her, to talk to her about his past. He needed to do that now. He needed to confess that Simon Singer had told Rachel and Mr. Schwartz everything he could remember about his life. But there was much he could not remember anymore. His mother could help him untangle his threads, mend the rips in his memory, heal the hurt in his heart.

But she had so many other worries right now, so many other things to think about. As soon as they got a letter, though . . .

A piercing whistle sliced the hot August air, causing everyone on the playground, students and teachers alike, to cover their ears. Since her cavernous, cave-like bus barn classroom had no bells, Miss Oxley, who disdained manmade whistles, simply squeezed her lower lip together with her fingers and shrieked her class into submission whenever the need arose.

"Make a straight line in the quickest of time!" bellowed Sadie Oxley, who specialized in original jingles. Her class didn't have to wait long to hear her all-time favorite: "Lack of attention will lead to detention!"

Rachel, the playground-elected jingle monitor, crossed her arms and held up two fingers where Miss Oxley could not see them but everybody else could. They wanted to laugh, but nobody dared.

"She catches you numbering her jingles, your name'll be the first one on the board," Simon whispered as he sidled up behind her. "Didn't learn much last year, did you, Rachel Elizabeth?"

"You're right," she said, quickly dropping her arms to her sides. "I got to be able to watch Agnes Ann's every move both before and after school! She'll sit at the back of the room, like always. We're going to have to take turns going to the pencil sharpener so we can look back and be sure she's there. She might sneak out when we're not looking!"

"Nobody sneaks out on Miss Oxley, Rachel.

Harry Houdini couldn't slip past her! As long as we're at school, Agnes Ann's being watched! By the way, Kenneth finally got here. He's last in line—and tracking."

"Forward, march!" Miss Oxley commanded as if she were leading the Forty-fifth Division into battle instead of the sixth-grade class of 1942-43 into their final year of grade school.

CHAPTER 21
The Wisdom of Solomon

"The three months since you were last in this classroom have brought many changes in the progress of the war," Miss Oxley said to begin the new school year. She picked up her yardstick and vigorously slapped random spots on the gigantic map hanging from a rack on the north wall. The tin wall behind the map vibrated ominously.

"We are going to do a great deal of map work this year," she added, whirling around to face them before a single groan could escape without her being able to note the mouth it came from. "We shall start with a detailed study of a section in the South Pacific north of Australia and west of New Guinea. The fighting there seems to intensify every day. Captain Midnight has informed us it is a geographical site that bears a great deal of watching."

She picked up a stack of papers and walked to the first desk of each of the five rows, counting out eight sheets per row.

"Pass the papers back, and you'll get no flak!" she cried, obviously pleased to use one of the "Words of War" she had written on the blackboard before they came in. "These are maps of the area we will be studying, but as you see, there are no names—only outlines. Do *not* get out your map pencils until you have been instructed to do so," she warned, narrowing her eyes at Rachel, who had already flipped opened her box and started to arrange the pencils at the top of her desk. Rachel quickly scooped the pencils back into the box and shoved it back in her desk while a blush that matched her hair spread across her face.

"This vast expanse of ocean," Miss Oxley continued, as she circled a large area on the map toward the bottom with her stick, "contains a number of islands whose names you will be expected to identify. Therefore, you will need to learn how to spell them correctly. Misspell a word, you're a dirty bird!" she trilled before she commanded, "Notebooks out! Pencils in position! Get ready to copy these words!"

She whirled around to face them once more, one end of her yardstick now gripped in her right fist and the length of it propped against her shoulder like a rifle. She stood at attention for a moment before she lowered the yardstick to her desk and picked up her chalk.

"And when you have finished copying each and every word," she shifted her eyes toward Rachel again, "then and only then may you get out your map pencils and begin to color." Miss Oxley squinted her eyes at a waving hand at the back of the room and let a full ten seconds pass before she inquired, "What possible question could you have, Agnes Ann? We haven't been in class long enough to engender any questions!"

"Who we fightin' down there, Hitler and those Nazis or the Japanese?"

Rachel whipped around to look at Agnes Ann so quickly she almost snapped a crick in her neck, but Simon kept his eyes glued to the map. At one time, in the past few months, his father's ship had been sailing that vast expanse of the Pacific Ocean Miss Oxley had just circled. He took it as a sign, a very good sign, that she would start their year with a study of that area. Maybe, he thought, he could learn something that could actually help his father. Something he could tell him about in a letter!

"No, Agnes Ann, to my knowledge, Hitler has no forces in the Pacific Theater. It's the Japanese navy we are engaging there. But surprisingly enough, that was an appropriate and intelligent question. I appreciate appropriate and intelligent questions."

Rachel scrunched down in her seat and began to chew on her eraser. In the first five minutes of the sixth grade she'd already managed to make Miss Oxley mad at her, and stupid Agnes Ann had asked an "appropriate and intelligent question."

Didn't Miss Oxley know the only possible reason Agnes Ann asked that question was because she wanted to know if swastikas would be appearing in the sand on those islands to scare our sailors? Rachel tried to get Simon's attention, but he was too busy squinting at the blackboard to notice. She wanted to use her foot-tapping signals from Captain Midnight's booklet on communication, but since she was on the first row as always, she didn't dare.

Simon closed his eyes and willed his father's ship to move somewhere near one of the islands Miss Oxley was now listing on the board. He'd seen a magician do that once, close his eyes and make a bottle move clear across the table. He visualized his father's ship moving toward one of those islands, an island whose name he would soon be able to spell and recognize.

He slipped his pencil out of his new red, white, and blue cardboard pencil box and began to copy down the names: Australia, New Guinea, New Britain, Guadalcanal, Savo Island, the Solomon Islands.

Solomon! That was it! The name he'd been trying to remember ever since he found that prayer shawl in the basement! Solomon! That was the name of his doll, the doll Hannah was taking care of for him. Solomon! Another sign, another really good sign! All he needed now was one more sign. Good signs always came in threes. That's what his father always said! What could the third one be? Simon slumped down in his desk as Agnes Ann shuffled by on her way to the pencil sharpener.

"Nebuchadnezzar!" she hissed at Rachel as she passed her desk. Miss Oxley was at the back of the room trying to help Stanley Wright get his pencil box open and didn't hear her. "King of the Jews!" Agnes Ann baited, but Rachel didn't look up or react at all. One mess-up a day was enough. The intelligent question asker was *not* going to drag her into detention.

"King of the Jews," Agnes Ann taunted again as she returned to her seat.

"King of the Jews?" Simon echoed in a whisper. Solomon was King of the Jews! Since signs were coincidences, one name the same as another, one word that goes with another, then Agnes Ann's riddle had just given him the third sign! John Alan was right. Nobody—not even Agnes Ann Billingsly—was all bad! She was a Hank Greenberg fan, wasn't she? She didn't *know* she was giving him the sign he needed, but she'd done it! He'd have to thank her for that at recess. If he could do it without Rachel sticking her nose in. He liked Rachel, but at times she sure could be a pest.

Simon sat up straight, opened his map pencil box, and took out the gold one. He drew a very large king's crown over the word Solomon and put a different-colored jewel on each of the crown's points before he began to color his map.

They would get a letter this very day, he decided as his map grew more and more colorful. Three great signs meant three important things were about to happen! They'd get a letter, they'd catch whoever was drawing the swastikas, and he'd finally be able to talk to his mother, tell her about everything that had happened since the day John Alan Feester left for California. No more secrets. He would tell her about the swastikas and about how he'd thought the saboteurs might be coming for him. He'd tell his mother all of it.

Except for the postcard.

She would want to do something about the postcard, to find those hungry people, to send them something of bread. And there was no way that could be done.

Simon was happy when Miss Oxley picked Rachel to take the attendance slip to the principal's office during recess, but no happier than Rachel was since it showed Miss Oxley wasn't really mad at her after all. Simon watched her saunter slowly across the playground, and when she rounded the corner, he quickly sidled over to Agnes Ann who, as she had all of last year, stood alone next to the building, her arms crossed in front of her and a big frown on her face.

"See that article about Hank Greenberg in *Life* magazine?" he asked as if the two of them talked about baseball every recess. "The one about how great he's doing in the Army Air Corps?" He braced himself for her usual opening salvo about his poor eyesight and thick glasses.

"Yeah, I saw it," she replied, dropping her arms and cocking her head to one side, obviously suspicious of his sudden burst of friendliness. "Maybe he'll win a medal or something. You like Hank the

Hammer?" she asked in an almost cheerful, certainly interested tone of voice. "That's what I call him, Hank the Hammer!"

"Sure, I even ..." He started to say he'd seen Greenberg play, but he didn't have time to go into that. If he didn't hurry, Rachel would be coming back and interrupting. "I ... I ..." Now that he had Agnes Ann's attention, he couldn't think of how to explain what he was going to say. "I just wanted to thank you for asking that riddle!" he blurted out. "It was a good one. A good riddle, that is, and it came along at just the right time, too!"

"At just the right time?" she eyed him carefully, trying to decide if he were making fun of her or not. "At just the right time?" she repeated.

"I ... I was looking for a sign," he explained, shrugging his shoulders as if that motion explained something. "I already had Miss Oxley picking the South Pacific, and then there was Solomon, from the Solomon Islands, you know, but I'd forgotten Solomon was a king of the Jews until you reminded me by talking about another king of the Jews. And that made my third sign. So—I just wanted to thank you, that's all."

"A third sign? Got no idea what you're talking about, Simon Green, but, up till right now, there's only been one person in the world who ever thanked me for doing anything, so I guess I'm supposed to say, 'You're welcome,' aren't I?" She narrowed her eyes at him again and then smiled. Simon had never seen Agnes Ann smile, and he was very surprised at how white and perfectly straight her teeth were.

"You got really pretty teeth, Agnes Ann. You ought to smile more often," he told her, glancing nervously over her shoulder to see if he could spot Rachel.

"Never got anything to smile about," she muttered in a flat tone. "That's the way it is when you got no friends here. When nobody in the whole sixth grade likes you." This sudden confession surprised him so much that he couldn't think of an appropriate reply. Agnes Ann worked so hard at being mean and cantankerous, he'd just assumed she didn't want any friends. He certainly hadn't thought about it being the other way around. And what did she mean by saying she had no friends *here*? Did she have friends somewhere else?

"You know the answer, don't you?" she went on, scuffing her cowboy boots back and forth and raising little puffs of dust in the process. "To my riddle, I mean. I hear you know everything."

"The answer is *that*, of course. T-h-a-t. But

Nebuchadnezzar wasn't the King of the Jews," he couldn't stop himself from pointing out, even though time was short. He paused before he added, "It makes a nice rhyme, however, and in riddles that counts more than accuracy, I guess."

"I guess," Agnes Ann repeated, returning his shrug. She smiled again.

Simon was so confused by this new Agnes Ann, he couldn't think of anything else to say. He wanted to ask her who the other person was who thanked her and what was he—or she—thanking her for, but he didn't have the nerve to do that. So he just strolled back toward Daddy Warbucks' to wait for Rachel's return.

He stopped at the first tree he came to and leaned against it. Taking a deep breath and letting it out very slowly, he watched Agnes Ann, who had refolded her arms, pasted the frown back on her face, and was glaring at a group of girls who were giggling and playing jump rope.

He was sorry she wasn't smiling. Agnes Ann really did have a pretty smile.

CHAPTER 22
News and Revelations

Simon heard the violin even before he turned the corner leading to his house, and he upended both of the geranium pots on the porch rail in his rush to the front door. His mother was making music again!

"We got a letter, didn't we?" he bellowed as he stampeded into the living room. "We got a letter from Dad! I knew it, I knew it, I knew it!" he yelled as he grabbed her in a bear hug.

"Mighty good thing I heard those thundering hooves of yours, partner," his mother drawled like one of the many cowboys he imitated. "Gave me time to fling my fiddle down. Otherwise, we'd be gluing pieces together till the cows come home!" She waved the letter in the air above her head and yelled, "*Yeeee-haw*! Read 'em, cowboy!"

"He's safe! He's not hurt! I knew it! I knew we'd get a letter today, too! Solomon said so, and Solomon's the wisest man who ever lived!"

"Solomon? The 'Wisdom of Solomon' king? You spoke with him personally? Will wonders never cease! Hold that story until after you read this letter! I should've waited for you, but I didn't! Actually, I've read it about a hundred times, but I'm ready for you to read it to me again!" She handed him the single sheet of blue V-mail.

Simon tried not to look disappointed at the thin flatness of the letter, but he couldn't help remembering the fat envelopes they received almost every day when his father was still stateside. They weren't just ordinary letters, but page after page of stories: funny stories, sad stories, made-up stories, real stories. The kind of stories only his father could write. But now their man of many words was restricted to a single sheet.

"It's dated the tenth of July!" his mother enthused, trying, as she always did, to make Simon feel better. "Only took a month to get here this time! This new V-mail's wonderful!"

Simon nodded enthusiastically, even though they

both knew a letter that old could have been written by a man who had been wounded by now, wounded or even killed. The Stones had gotten a letter from their son several months after he'd been reported killed in action.

"Come on, Simon, read! One more time and I'll have it memorized!" She plopped back on the couch, hugged a pillow to her chest, and closed her eyes to listen.

"'My Scintillating Sylvia and Simon Says Son,'" Simon began.

"Alliterative music to my ears," his mother declared, opening her eyes and sitting up to study his face. "Your voice! It's starting to sound just like your father's, Simon! I never noticed that before! Read on! Read on! 'My love is winging its way . . .' comes next."

"'My love is winging its way from I can't say where to your waiting hearts, but as your eyes follow the old familiar hen scratching scrawled across this page, you will have no doubt the writing is mine and that I still have all my fingers. Toes, too. In fact all my parts are fine and in working order! I know that's the news you are always waiting to hear.

"'I am well and well fed. I have received your many letters. They nestle in my pillow so I can go to sleep each night and awaken each morning with your words, your thoughts, and your love slipping from the pages straight into my head.

"'Much to do today, so this letter must be short, but my love is long, long and eternal for my beautiful wife and my handsome and brilliant son! Take care of each other and, as they say on that most decadent of instruments, the cursed radio, 'Keep them cards and letters coming!'

"'Now that you've fessed up to rotting your brains on a daily basis, I picture you both sinking in a quagmire of soap operas. Nevertheless, I love you and plan to enjoy rescuing the both of you!

"'Izzy ... better known as Dad.'"

"Better known as Dad," Sylvia repeated, biting her lip and fighting back her tears. "That's the title he cherishes most, you know that, Simon? Not novelist, not journalist, but Dad! I never knew a man who wanted to be a father more than he did!"

"I know," Simon said, rubbing his fingers over his father's signature and trying not to think about the signature on the postcard. "Not a word blacked!" he boasted, sticking the letter under her nose as if she hadn't seen it yet and steering the conversation away from the subject of fatherhood. "Rachel says lots of the letters they get are all blacked out, but those censors wouldn't dare cancel a word of Isadore

Green, famous novelist! Against the rules of the Geneva Convention, I bet!"

"Your salty old dad knows the rules of writing. 'Loose lips' not only sink ships but sink words right out of letters, too. It's totally possible that the censor's an admirer of your father's writing. Thousands of them floating around, according to his fan mail. That's what his editor says anyway. Glad they're holding them in New York for The Duration. That basement of ours is not big enough to hold mail sacks. They say they've got dozens of them!"

The subject of mail followed so closely by the mention of the basement made Simon drop his eyes and bite his lip, but his mother was too excited to notice.

"Now," she said, grabbing both his hands and pulling him into the kitchen. "Eat your snack and tell me all about this visit you had with wise King Solomon before it's time for ..." She lowered her voice in order to imitate the smooth-as-chocolate-milk radio announcer, "The next exciting episode of radio's 'Captain Midnight!'"

"Hey, you're pretty good at that," Simon said between bites of his jelly sandwich and sips of Ovaltine. "If the regular guy ever decides to quit, I'll get the Captain to hire you!"

He grinned at her and tried to decide how to

begin. Now that they had gotten a letter, he could tell her his story, but he couldn't do it by becoming Simon Singer again as he had done for Rachel and Mr. Schwartz. Simon Green was the only person who could play this part.

"Well, first I'll tell you how I knew we got a letter. It's really pretty funny. Funny as in *strange,* not funny as in 'ha ha!'" he started, picking his words slowly and carefully. "You remember how Dad's always looking for 'signs,' especially after he's mailed a manuscript off? He'll look for a 'sign' to tell him his article will sell, a 'sign' that he's about to land a book contract. Remember?"

"Ah, yes, Isadore Green and his famous signs," his mother sighed as she shook her head and gazed out the window. "When his agent was trying to sell his first book, we went to a party where we didn't know a single soul in the room, and the first three people we were introduced to had the same names as characters in his book! Not ordinary names like Sue or Jane or Bill, either. Nope, they were Emmaline, Winston, and even Alphonzo, for goodness' sake! Well, your old dad decided immediately that was a 'sign' the book would sell. And sure enough, one week later, he got the letter. The book had sold while we were at that party!"

"Three in a row! That's what Dad says it takes!"

Simon drained his glass. "More Ovaltine, please," he demanded holding up his glass and parroting the kid on the radio commercial. He was glad she had a story to tell, too. They could exchange stories, he and his mother. That would make being Simon Green again much easier.

"Your wish is my command," she laughed, pouring the milk with the flourish of a waiter in a fancy restaurant and spooning the Ovaltine in as if it were a magic potion.

"My mother the genie! Well, my signs weren't as obvious as those three names, but they were *signs* all right! First of all, Miss Oxley says we're going to be doing lots of map work, and the part of the map we started with is right where Dad was headed the last time we heard anything. Out of all the whole world, she picks the spot I think he might be in! Then, the second sign came to me the day John Alan moved away, but I didn't know it was a sign then. I found that out today. It . . . has to do with Solomon and him being a Jewish king, which was the *third* sign. Kind of, anyway." He felt his mouth getting dry, so he stopped to take a long sip of Ovaltine before he asked, "You remember that old trunk, the one Dad said to put in the basement and forget?"

"The one with books and manuscripts? Sure, I

remember. It weighs a ton and a half! I did exactly what he told me to do, put it in the basement and forgot about it."

"Well, I forgot about it, too. Until I decided I needed a present for John Alan. I wanted a stupendous, glorious going-away present, like a rare and wonderful Babe Ruth baseball card!"

"Well, I'm glad about that. Especially since he gave you his stupendous, glorious, wonderful bicycle! But ... you didn't know about that bike at the time he was leaving," she said slowly. "You didn't get that bike until several days after he left."

"Right! Anyhow, I looked every place I could think of in the house, but I couldn't find that card. Then I remembered the trunk and decided to look in there. Well," he slowed his story down, "I ... didn't find the Babe Ruth card, but I did ... I did find a couple of other things that belong to me." He stopped and put his hands on top of hers, which were resting on the table. "Actually, it was a couple of other things that belonged to Simon Singer."

At the sound of that long unspoken name, Sylvia caught her breath and sat up very straight. She slipped her palms over so she could grip both of his hands in hers. It was the first time he had spoken Simon Singer's name since the day Isadore made him promise to forget his past, the very first time he had spoken aloud the name which had been his for the first six years of his life.

"And ... and what were these things of Simon Singer's?" she asked, and he could tell she was trying very hard to regulate her breathing. "These things of *yours*, I mean."

Simon let got of her hands and went over to the bottom kitchen drawer, where he had hidden the handkerchief and the napkin prayer shawl under a stack of recipe books. He took the two pieces of cloth out and spread them on the table in front of her.

"When I saw these again," he said, looking into Sylvia's green eyes, now sparkling with tears, "the prayer shawl I made for my Solomon doll and the handkerchief my Polish grandmother embroidered with my initials ... when I saw them, I remembered."

"Remembered what, sweet Simon Says?" she whispered so softly he had to lean closer to understand what she was asking.

"Bits and pieces. Big bits, little pieces ... of that other life ... my life as Simon Singer. And I need to talk to you about it, to see what you remember, to know what was in the letters the man named Max wrote to you, to know what was in the papers the

man named Max brought with him. And ... and ..."
he was talking faster now, "I need to tell you what
finding Simon Singer's things caused me to do ...
who I had to tell about that other life of mine."

"Oh, Simon," she said, going over to wrap her
arms around him. "I knew this day would come. I
was never sure we had done the right thing, asking
you to wipe out six years of your life, asking you to
forget you had been a boy named Simon Singer. But
Izzy thought ... he wanted so very badly to be your
real father, for me to be your real mother, and I love
him so much, so very much!"

"But that's just it! He *is* my real father! And you
are my real mother! But still ... there are those other
people, the ones who are—"

"I know, Simon, I know. And I'll do all I can to
help you. We'll talk about it all, and I will try to help
you understand." She pulled him into the living
room and sat down on the sofa next to him. "Now,
we'll both start at the beginning. I'll tell you everything I remember, and you can tell me what you
remember and ... and ... it's going to be *okay,*
Simon! I promise you, it is going to be *okay!*"

Simon grabbed both her hands and squeezed her
fingers very hard.

"You're trying to make me squeal, aren't you?"

she smiled through her tears. "That's what *real* mothers do, isn't it?"

He nodded. It was all going to be okay.

"Real mothers squeal," she repeated, "and ... real mothers find lost baseball cards, too!"

"They find what?"

"They find lost baseball cards. Your Babe Ruth card! It's in my jewelry box! You gave it to me to keep for you because it was so precious. Ask any mother, she'll tell you. One of a mother's most solemn duties is to keep track of her son's baseball cards." She mussed his hair as she added, "If she's a *real* mother, that is!"

CHAPTER 23
Schwartz's Many Secrets

As far as Simon and the other people who were scanning the ground for the swastikas could determine, two whole weeks went by without another Nazi symbol appearing anywhere in town. That fact, along with the great relief he felt after discussing Simon Singer with his mother, made Simon's life as tolerable as it could be with the country at war and his father on a ship sailing toward an unknown destination. He didn't tell Rachel about his talk with Agnes Ann. As Mr. Schwartz pointed out, everybody is entitled to have secrets of one kind or another.

During the two-week lull, Simon received his first letter from John Alan Feester in care of Mr.

Schwartz. It arrived a whole week before Rachel got one addressed to their Secret Squadron. Simon's letter, of course, was much more personal, much more private. He stayed in the back of Schwartz's Meat Market reading the news of John Alan's long, hot trip to California several times before he folded it up and hid it in his pants pocket.

Both letters had a permanent return address, so while Rachel publicly drafted a reply from the group, Simon secretly gathered his courage and crept back down into the basement. He opened the trunk only long enough to grab his *Wind in the Willows* off the top layer where he'd left it and slam the lid shut again. He sang "California, Here I Come" to keep from hearing the hungry people call Simon Singer's name, but it didn't work very well. For the first time in years, that night he dreamed about Simon Singer's family.

The next day he mailed *Wind in the Willows,* along with its rare and wonderful Babe Ruth bookmark, to the very best friend he'd ever had, wishing with all his heart he could also be mailing something of bread to the hungry people.

Simon persuaded Mr. Schwartz to tell Rachel about the swastika outside his shop's back door but not to mention that Simon was in the shop while the swastika was being drawn.

"What Rachel doesn't know, won't hurt me!" Simon assured the bemused butcher. "She'd want to know every word we said, every detail of what happened, and I figure you and me and Hank Greenberg need our privacy, don't we?"

"Hank Greenberg most of all," Mr. Schwartz chuckled.

When Rachel marched outside the butcher shop to inspect the "scene of the crime," as she insisted on calling it, she immediately noticed the easy access to the bone box and demanded that Mr. Schwartz make a list of people who came for the free bones.

"But Rachel, I have no idea who comes to get them. I put them out, they disappear. That's all I know about it."

"Well, then, the Secret Squadron needs to have a meeting tomorrow to discuss possible suspects," she insisted. "Can we have it in the back of your store? Pretty please? We can't have it at my house or Kenneth's because Simon doesn't want anybody else to know about this. Simon wants privacy when he's talking about swastikas and Nazis, you know," she added in a whisper, since Simon had told her Mr. Schwartz knew the secret of Simon Singer also.

"Simon has trusted you with a very important confidence, Rachel," Mr. Schwartz cautioned her. "A confidence as important as the one concerning the brick thrown through the window of Sam Sing's laundry, in fact."

Rachel's eyes got very big. She thought she and Paul were the only two people in the world who knew the truth about that brick other than Mr. Snow, who threw it, and Mr. Sing himself. Was this Mr. Schwartz's way of telling her that he knew, too? He *knew* and hadn't told anybody? Even her father, editor of the newspaper, didn't know who threw that brick!

"Sam Sing is my friend, Rachel, my very good friend. He's the only Chinese in our town, and Mrs. Schwartz and I are the only Jews. Or were until Simon and his mother came. When Mr. Snow came and confessed to Sam Sing, explained he had only thrown the brick out of fear that his grandsons would have to go to war, Sam forgave him. Sam told me of your kindness in wanting to protect them both, your good heart. That is why I know you are worthy of Simon's trust as well as mine in telling you this story."

"Loose lips sink ships." Rachel nodded. "And I wouldn't sink Mr. Snow or Simon's ships for anything in the world."

"Mr. Snow knows that, and you know that, and I know that. But it would do nobody any good at all for the rest of the town to know that. Some secrets must be kept forever."

She shook her head solemnly, then crossed her heart and hoped to die. She was very glad her mother wasn't around to see her do it.

The Secret Squadron rode their bikes to Schwartz's Meat Market after they finished listening to Captain Midnight, but they had to wait to begin their meeting until Mr. Schwartz closed for the day.

"Maybe Agnes Ann's still drawing them and somebody else is finding them and rubbing them out before we see them!" Rachel mused as they listened to Mr. Schwartz explain to an irate customer why there was such a small selection of meat on Friday.

"Or, maybe she's noticed that one of the three of us is watching her every move," Simon added. "Or, maybe ... just maybe ... *she* is not a *she* at all!"

"Oh, she's a *she,* all right! It's Agnes Ann Billingsly! I'd bet my Captain Midnight Code-O-Graph badge on that!"

"Guilty until proven innocent!" Kenneth intoned, giving one loud rap on the barrel top with the wooden meat hammer Mr. Schwartz had left lying there. "So says Rachel Elizabeth Dalton, both judge and jury!"

"Well, it seems pretty coincidental to me that the day school starts, the very day we start watching her like a hawk, the drawings stop! How do you explain that, huh? It's been two whole weeks!"

"Circumstantial, my dear Watson, purely circumstantial," Simon drawled in his Sherlock Holmes voice as the bell on the front door jingled and the lock clicked to signal the closing of the shop.

"Any new swastikas to report?" Mr. Schwartz inquired as he strolled into the back room, removing his apron as he came through the door.

"Not unless they're getting erased before we see them," Rachel replied.

"Well, perhaps no news is good news. Your vigilance seems to have stopped the artist for the time being. By the way, Kenneth, speaking of artist, how's my friend Gus feeling? Gus trades me pictures of his dog for bones, you know. Mrs. Schwartz has covered the walls with them! Such a talent he is. How old is he now, three, four? I heard the chickenpox caught him."

"He's four, but he thinks he's old enough to enlist! Last month, when we were shopping in Lawton, he wandered off, and I found him on the lap of an army recruiter! The guy was teaching him to play 'Simon Says!'" Kenneth pointed a finger at

Simon and grinned. "That recruiter told us the military actually has used that game with trainees to see if they can remember how to obey commands. Gus is all well now. Actually, he's been feeling good since last week, but our grandmother wouldn't let him out of her sight until today. She was sure he'd have a relapse or scratch a pox and get a scar. You know my Taci."

"Ah, yes, I know your grandmother," Mr. Schwartz mused. "She was the first person to befriend us when we came to this town. Did I ever tell you that? Back before statehood even. Your grandmother brought us our supper that first night, buffalo meat and roasted corn. My bride Ruthie had never seen an Indian. When your grandmother came to our door, wrapped in her colorful blanket, a papoose cradle on her back and long braids hanging down, Ruthie actually ran to me for protection! Ruthie, who could have easily passed for a Kiowa herself with her high cheekbones, her lovely Roman nose, her shiny black hair! Oh, my, so young she was! So young and foolish!"

"Mrs. Schwartz was afraid of my grandmother?" Kenneth asked incredulously. "*My* Taci?"

"People are often afraid of those who are different from them, until the differences turn out to be similarities. Your Taci taught me how to butcher a buffalo! We called our method 'Kiowa kosher.' What a time we had in those early days!" He chuckled as he hung his apron on the hook and removed his straw hat from the rack.

"And who was the papoose in the cradle on my grandmother's back?" Kenneth wanted to know. "What was the year?"

"Nineteen one. And the baby is now your grown-up Uncle Bob, the forty-year-old military doctor!" He put his hat on and flipped off the light in the front. "Now, Simon, I will leave you in charge of locking up when your meeting is over. Follow me now and lock the door behind me. It gets very hot back here if you close the wooden door, so I'll leave it open so you can get what little breeze there is through the screen. Be sure to close and bolt it before you leave. And pull the chain on this light. Drop the key at my house on your way home. I must hurry! Mrs. Schwartz has promised me gefilte fish and hot challah bread for supper!" he explained as he headed out the door. He winked at Kenneth as he added, "Gefilte fish is almost as good as Kiowa kosher buffalo!"

When Simon returned from locking the door, Rachel began. "Well, gentlemen, here are the facts as we know them. The first two swastikas appeared on the floor of Daddy Warbucks' mansion. On both occasions Agnes Ann Billingsly, Public Enemy Number

One, was in or around the vicinity of the mansion. Simon and I can both testify to that."

"I could swear she rode by on her bike, Rachel, but I hardly think Agnes Ann deserves to have her picture on the wall at the post office," Simon countered. "She's not exactly Bonnie Parker, you know."

"What we *know* is that the third swastika appeared right outside the back door of this shop," Rachel droned on, ignoring his reply. "We also know that the box where Agnes Ann Billingsly picks up bones for Spike is on the shelf right above where the swastika was drawn. Therefore," she swept the air with her left arm and pointed her index finger with her right, "the evidence is overwhelming that Agnes Ann Billingsly is our culprit!"

"Rachel," Simon protested, "you said we were going to talk about facts! The fact is every kid with a bike rides past those trees, and those who don't have bikes walk by them. You heard Mr. Schwartz say lots of people get those bones. You get them for Jeep, Kenneth gets them for Spot. Lots of other people get them for lots of other dogs."

"Yes, but I don't draw swastikas and Kenneth doesn't draw swastikas, and none of those other people have any reason to draw swastikas! Agnes Ann's mad about the war. She likes to stir up trouble. She's very prejudiced. She's a bad person, just like her father!"

"Lots of people are mad about the war, Rachel. Simon's right. You don't have any evidence that Agnes Ann is drawing the swastikas," Kenneth said, shaking his head. "No footprints on the ground, no article of clothing left behind, nothing! Believe me, I want to find whoever's drawing those things just as bad as you do. Those Nazis stole our sacred symbol, and the idea that somebody is drawing it in the dirt to stir up trouble, to get people riled up—"

He was interrupted by a loud crash outside the screen door, followed by an even louder yell and the barking of a dog.

Rachel, followed closely by Simon and Kenneth, bolted to the screen door. They all three shoved it open at the same time.

There, on the ground, was another giant swastika.

And lying next to it, a drawing stick in one hand and a bone in the other, was Gus Stumbling Bear.

CHAPTER 24
Gus Tells His Secret

"But Gus, where did you *see* what you drew on the ground over there?" Kenneth asked the four-year-old once it was determined that only Gus' pride had been hurt in his fall. Kenneth asked the question in a casual tone, but Rachel and Simon could hear the puzzlement and anger in his voice. The three of them stood around in a circle studying the swastika as if they had never seen one before.

"In Taci's sewing basket!" Gus piped up, happy to be the center of attention of a trio of older kids. "She gots bunches of little red squares, all the same. All with that," he pointed to the swastika, "in yellow in their middles!" He lowered his voice to a whisper.

"There's some on her *secret* shawl! Her *secret* shawl is way in the back of the closet. She never lets anybody see it." His sparkling brown eyes grew wide as he asked again, "You know about her *secret* shawl, Kenneth? You ever see it? I think this—" he pointed at the swastika, "is a secret sign!"

"Yes, I've seen the secret shawl, little brother," Kenneth replied, pulling gently on the little boy's braids, first the right and then the left, causing Gus' head to shake back and forth. "I've seen those patches of Uncle Bob's, too," Kenneth added, looking up at Rachel and Simon and shrugging his shoulders. "But I sure didn't know you'd seen them. Grandmother took those patches off not very long before you were born. I thought they'd been thrown away."

"You like my secret sign, Simon?" Gus asked, standing up so he could get a better view of his artwork. "Kenneth taught me how to make an 'S' with straight lines. Snakes are harder." He drew another swastika, smaller this time, and added a series of squared-off S's across the ground.

"Yep, I taught you everything you know, little brother," Kenneth sighed. "But there are a few things I guess I should've taught you that I didn't." He glanced first at Simon and then at Rachel, before he added, "Tell you what, little brother, let's erase

214

this secret sign so Mr. Schwartz won't think we are people who . . . who make messes."

"But Kenneth, Mr. Schwartz knows I don't make messes! He tells me I am a fine artist! I made him this picture of Spot to pay for this bone!" Gus went over to Simon, who was sitting on the step giving Spot's ears a good scratching. The little boy pulled a very wrinkled piece of paper from his pocket and flattened it out on the step. "See, in this picture Spot is peeing on a salt block in Mr. Schwartz's store! That's a funny picture, isn't it? It makes me laugh." He put his hand over his mouth and chortled. Then he looked around and lowered his voice as he added, "Spot did that one day, but Mr. Schwartz didn't see him do it. Don't tell him, okay?"

Kenneth, glad to have something to smile about, kept a straight face as he knelt in front of Gus. "Did Spot really pee on Mr. Schwartz's salt block?"

"Yes, but he didn't mean to, and he was very sorry," Gus said, shaking his head up and down this time. His face brightened as he added, "Spot picked a yellow block instead of a white one, but I am still sure he didn't *mean* to pee on it!"

Rachel and Simon both had to put their hands over their mouths to stifle their laughter, but Kenneth was able to contain himself.

"Don't tell Mr. Schwartz," Gus whispered. "He might get mad at Spot and stop giving him bones."

"But Gus, don't you think maybe when Mr. Schwartz sees your picture, he might wonder where you got such an idea and go check on his salt blocks?" Simon wanted to know.

"Not unless you tell him to look, Simon. Everybody has to do what *you* say, so don't you tell him."

"They do?" Simon asked in mock amazement. "Everybody? Even Rachel? Even Kenneth? Even you? Everybody has to do what I say?"

"If they don't want to get put out of the army," Gus explained, making fists out of both hands and pointing his thumbs to the sky. "Whatever Simon says is what everybody has to do. I learned that when I joined the army! If Simon says I have to tell Mr. Schwartz about Spot peeing on the yellow salt block, then I have to tell him, or I'm out of the army."

"Okay," Simon said, drawing the word out slowly as he scratched Gus and Spot both on the head at the same time. "I tell you what, Gus. We need to play a little game of Simon Says right now."

"Can Spot play, too?"

"Sure, Spot can play. So can Kenneth and Rachel. Now here's what Simon says. Everybody listen very carefully so you won't get put out of the army." He grinned at Rachel, who stuck her tongue out at him. "*Nobody* wants to get put out of the army, right?"

Gus put both arms around Spot's neck and whispered in his ear, "You listen, Spot, so we won't get put out of the army."

Simon spoke slowly and seriously. "Simon says nobody can draw the secret 'S' sign ever again anymore. Not on the ground, not on a piece of paper, not on a wall. Not anywhere at all."

"Not *ever*?" Gus asked incredulously. "But it's my best secret picture!"

"You don't want to get put out of the army, do you, little brother?" Kenneth asked, slapping Simon on the back with one hand and rubbing Gus on the head with the other.

"No," Gus admitted. "I don't want to get put out of the army, Kenneth."

"Then all you got to remember is that you don't draw the secret 'S' anymore anywhere and you get to stay in the army."

"Until I get to be a general?"

"Until you get to be a general," Kenneth assured him, "or for The Duration, whichever comes first ..."

CHAPTER 25
Home from California

"Well, go ahead and say it, Simon," Rachel sighed after Kenneth had written out an IOU to Mr. Schwartz for one salt block and left to take Gus and Spot home for supper. "I'm a twit who ought to get her facts straight. The fact is no swastikas were drawn for two weeks because Gus had chickenpox and couldn't leave the house to draw them! The fact is Gus is so short nobody could see him running down the alley to Mr. Schwartz's! I'm sure there's lots more facts I'll think of later. Go ahead, say it, Simon Says! Say, 'Simon says Rachel's a twit as well as a twerp!'"

"Aw, Rachel, I'm not going to rub it in. I know you. You'll be hard enough on yourself. But you'll have to admit you were wrong to find Agnes Ann guilty because you think her father's a black marketeer. You don't know for sure he's guilty either."

"But everybody in town thinks—"

"Everybody *thinks*, but they don't know. Mr. Billingsly hasn't been arrested for being a back marketeer, has never even been charged."

"You're right," she said, hanging her head and chewing her lower lip. "I'm glad you kept me from accusing Agnes Ann. I wanted to do it in front of people, to shame her publicly, and that would have been awful. Nobody likes her anyway, and if I'd done that, we would have had to tell the whole world it was really Gus. That would have been double awful for everybody we know!"

"Well, we can forget about it now. Kenneth's not going to tell, and Gus is so little if he said something people would think it was just another one of his war stories. The swastika episode can be one more military secret."

"I knew you were smart," Rachel replied as she picked up Gus' drawing stick and broke it in two, "but pulling Simon Says on Gus was the greatest idea since sliced bread! All you got to do is tell a little kid something's bad or naughty and shouldn't be said or drawn, and that's all they want to do. Because of you, Gus won't ever draw another swastika! He sure doesn't want to get kicked out of the army!"

"Well, Simon says it's time to lock up Mr. Schwartz's and go eat supper. When I drop his key off, I'll tell him the swastika mystery's been solved."

"Sure wish I could solve the missing Paul mystery," Rachel moaned as she got up to follow Simon back into the store. "Thought for sure he'd be back by now. Since he's already missed the first two weeks of school, I'm scared his father may have changed his mind again. This is the longest he's ever gone without writing us. I'm real worried about him, Simon. Real worried."

"I bet he's okay, Rachel," Simon assured her as he turned the key and jiggled the lock. "Ride with me to Mr. Schwartz's. It not far out of your way. Then I'll stop by your house and give Jeep his afternoon belly rub. Now that John Alan's gone, he likes me best, you know."

"Sure, sure, Simon, if *you* say so. Gus told us all about Simon Says!" she laughed. "Pump slow, I'm not in any hurry. Mama's probably already gone back down to the Legion Hall. Red Cross stuff, like always." She put one hand above her eyes and checked the street in both directions. "Paul's daddy's car was worn out before they left here for California.

They had to stop for water every other mile almost, and the tires were awful. They didn't have any tread at all! Can't imagine how bad they must be by now. I can just see them stalled out in the middle of that hot desert with nobody coming by to help them."

"Well, the war's got everybody moving so much, people are getting lots better about stopping to help each other. I read that in the paper last week. Said in America, anyway, the war's making everybody care about each other more, making good people out of bad."

"All except for Agnes Ann's black-marketeer father," Rachel snipped.

"Haven't you learned anything at all, Rachel? Nobody's all bad, not even the Billingslys." He took a deep breath before adding, "I know for a fact Agnes Ann's got some good in her. She's a Hank Greenberg fan! Any person who's a Hank Greenberg fan can't be all bad!"

"How would you know which baseball player Agnes Ann likes?" Rachel quizzed him, going into a coast so she could look at his face.

"Mr. Schwartz told me. Says he and Agnes Ann discuss baseball all the time. In fact, he was surprised to find out we think she's mean. He thinks she's pretty nice."

She started pumping again, faster now. "Agnes

Ann Billingsly? Nice? Agnes Ann's never been nice to anybody in her life!"

"She wishes she had some friends," Simon said, fixing his eyes on the sidewalk and pedaling faster to keep up.

"Did she tell Mr. Schwartz *that*, too?"

"No. She told me. The first day of school. When you were taking Miss Oxley's attendance report to the office. We had a quite a long conversation, Agnes Ann and I. She ... she has a real pretty smile."

Rachel didn't say anything the rest of the way to Mr. Schwartz's house, but she did wait for Simon at the end of the sidewalk while he gave the key back and told Mr. Schwartz their news. She saw Mr. Schwartz shake his head back and forth, but she couldn't hear what they were saying.

"How come you didn't tell me about any of this?" she asked when Simon was riding next to her again. "About you thinking Agnes Ann wanted friends, I mean."

"I ... I had a lot on my mind, remember? But I'm telling you now. I felt sorry for her, Rachel. I know what it's like to not have any friends. You don't. You've always had Paul and then John Alan. I don't know any kid in our class that doesn't like you. Except maybe for Agnes Ann."

"Well, she sure doesn't act like she wants friends. Calling Kenneth a redskin, making fun of our glasses, mouthing off at everybody all the time ..."

"I think that's all a front. Since people started not liking her because of her father, I think she decided just to not like them back. All of them."

"Do you honestly think if we ... if we ... well, I'm not at all sure what you want us to do about any of this, Simon, but I'm going to think about what you said. You've been lots more places, had lots more ... lots more experiences than I have."

They had just reached the corner of the sidewalk where she turned to her house and he turned to his when Rachel spotted a familiar scene.

"Oh, Simon, look! In my front yard! It's Paul! Bad as my eyes are, I know that has to be Paul! He's the only person in the world other than John Alan Feester that Jeep would jump six feet in the air to greet! It's Paul! He's home! Come on, Simon," Rachel cried, "race me home! Paul's waiting on us!"

CHAPTER 26
Pen Pals

"You're going to ruin your tires running over the grass like that. Don't you know there's a war on?" Paul laughed when Rachel and Simon both came skidding to a halt on the grass right in front of him. "Hey, Simon, haven't you learned better than to try to beat Rachel at anything?"

"But Paul, how come you didn't write and tell us you were on your way home?" Rachel exclaimed as she jumped off her bike and grabbed him in a bear hug. "You could have at least dropped us a penny postcard from somewhere!" When he didn't hug her back, just let his arms dangle at his side, she stepped back to inspect him more closely. "And what happened to your hair? Loopin' loops, Paul! You look like you got drafted!"

"It's called a crewcut," he said, running both hands over his head self-consciously. "Everybody in California has them. I . . . I knew you wouldn't like it, Rachel."

"I sure do," Simon said. "I've been trying to get my mom to let me get one, but so far no luck."

"Oh, it's okay, I guess," Rachel said, circling around him. "It'll just take some getting used to. And you're taller than me now!" she cried, turning back to back with him and putting her hand on his head. "Even with no hair! A whole bunch taller! How much, Simon? How much taller is he? I didn't know anybody could grow that much in nine months!"

"Babies do. Before they're born anyway," Paul grinned, winking at Simon. Rachel found herself blushing, but she wasn't sure why. "Hey, now your face matches your hair," Paul teased. "Has it always been that red? Your hair, I mean. No wonder Simon was always patting you on the head and scratching you behind the ears. That's what he claimed in his letters anyway. Said that Irish setter hair of yours made him miss his dog something awful! You write great letters, Simon."

"He never patted me on the hair or scratched my

ears," Rachel snapped, turning to look from one to the other. "He looked like he wanted to, but he never actually *did* it." She stared down at the ground and tried to think of what to say next. Never in her life had she had to *think* of what to say to Paul Griggs. Always before, she just said it. Why did things seem to be different now? Was it the fact that Simon was standing there?

"Hey, Simon, isn't that John Alan's bike?" Paul asked as he studied the bike more carefully. "Don't tell me he left his bike here!"

"He said he couldn't ride a bike in California. All that traffic you told us about in your letters ..." Simon shrugged. There was an awkward moment of silence before he added, "Hey, I'm sure the two of you have lots to talk about, and my mother's going to wonder where I am, so I'll head for home." He climbed back on his bike and prepared to take off. "Good to have you back, Paul. Rachel was about to get a search party out for you. See you at school tomorrow."

"I'm ... I'm glad he left, Paul," Rachel said when Simon was far enough away he couldn't hear her. "We've become really good friends, but ... but it's suppertime, and we don't have enough chairs for him." She brightened as she added, "But we've sure still got the one Daddy bought for you! Mama's already put it back where it belongs. We moved it away from the table the day you left." She started to grab his hand but changed her mind. "Seeing that empty chair, the one Daddy ordered especially for you, would have made us miss you even more."

"Yeah, I know what you mean," Paul said, now shifting from one foot to the other. "I'd forgotten about that chair. Speaking of supper, I'm starved! Chairs won't be a problem tonight. We'll be the only ones at the table. Your mom had to go do more Red Cross work. My mom went over to check on our house, your dad had to go back to the office, and Al's upstairs doing homework. He's our chaperone, I guess."

"Our chaperone? Why would we need a chaperone?" Rachel asked, genuinely puzzled by his last remark.

Paul didn't answer. He just followed her up the steps, but when they got to the porch, he didn't charge in front of her like he used to do. Instead he opened the door for her, bowed, and said, "Ladies first!" while Jeep almost bowled both of them over in his race to get inside.

"You still haven't said why you haven't written for a hundred years!" she said, poking him in the back as they made their way through the house with Jeep running circles around both of them.

"Wasn't gone a hundred years, Rachel, even though it seemed like it sometimes! And I didn't know when we were leaving until the day we left. Pop kept changing his mind. Then, when we finally hit Route 66, we kept having car trouble. Finally, just outside Amarillo, we had not one but two flat tires at the same time! That's when Pop just took off. You know Pop." He stopped to give Jeep a belly rub.

"Your father left you? Left you by the side of the road? I told Simon that's what was going to happen! I told him that today!"

"Well, we'd still be sitting there if it weren't for Jake Billingsly," Paul informed her as he abandoned Jeep to grab up a plate and begin filling it with potato salad, baked beans, coleslaw, and ham.

"Jake Billingsly?" Rachel cried. "What do you mean you'd still be there if it weren't for Jake Billingsly? What does Jake Billingsly have to do with anything?"

"He's the person who came to our rescue," Paul replied in a tone that sounded much too casual. Rachel had known him too long to not know when Paul Griggs was squirming about something. "Can't believe I lucked out like this! Your mother has all my favorite food! She said she had a feeling we'd be rolling in today. Woman's intuition, that's what it is."

Paul pretended to be so busy filling his plate he didn't notice the look Rachel was giving him, but she could see him watching her out of the corner of his eye.

"Want to tell me exactly how Jake Billingsly saved you, Mr. I've-Got-a-Secret?" she finally blurted out.

"Well, I know from what you said in your letters that since I left, everybody thinks Jake's become a black market guy," he said between bites. "Of course, I couldn't say anything about that one way or another. I remember people around here never liked him very much even before the war started. But I know for sure that he came through in a pinch for my mom and me. Drove all the way from here to Amarillo to bring us four new tires. Even put them on for us and wouldn't let us pay him anything!"

"Jake Billingsly did that? But why would he do that, Paul? How'd he even know you were in Amarillo?"

"Agnes Ann told him," Paul said, but this time he looked down at his plate instead of at her.

"Agnes Ann told him? How'd *she* know?"

"I . . . I called her," Paul stammered. "On the telephone."

"Long distance? You called Agnes Ann Billingsly long distance? Where'd you get the money? How'd you know her number?"

"I ... I called her collect. She put her telephone number in one of her letters and told me to use it. In case of an emergency. I carried that page of her letter with me all the time." He took another big bite of ham and chewed it very slowly.

One of her letters? Agnes Ann had been writing letters to Paul, and he had been answering her? With personal letters? Rachel wanted very badly to stop him, to demand that he tell her about those letters, but something held her back. She also wanted to point out that those tires were probably straight off the black market, that Jake Billingsly had no doubt gotten them illegally. But she was so amazed by Paul's story that she just waited for him to go on talking.

"Well, you see, Rachel," he said slowly, "when Miss Cathcart had the class make that birthday banner for me back in February ... remember that banner?"

"Sure I do. I was the one who told her about our Friday the 13th birthdays in February and March. It was *my* idea to send you a good luck banner!"

"Well, Agnes Ann was the one who mailed it to me. Miss Cathcart asked her to because she walks right by the post office on her way home." He began to talk faster now. "Well, you see ... Agnes Ann copied my address off the mailing tube and ... and ..." He shrugged as he added, "And she started writing me letters." He picked up his fork and began to count the tines.

"Agnes Ann started writing to you?" Rachel said very slowly as if she were memorizing a line for a play. "Agnes Ann wrote you letters?"

"She wrote me two or three times a week," Paul admitted. "Sometimes more. She really *likes* writing letters. Her letters, and the other ones I got," he quickly added, "the ones you all wrote me as a group, were the only thing that kept me from going nuts out there, Rachel. I wrote you about my Japanese friends, Max and Woody, being taken away to concentration camps. They wrote me, too, after they got over being so mad about being locked up for no reason at all. They're having a terrible time out there in the desert, a really terrible time. They're in prison, you know. Locked up like they'd committed a crime, when all they did was get born Japanese."

"I couldn't believe it when that happened, Paul. I tried to get my father to do something about it, write something in his newspaper, but he said there wasn't anything that could be done."

231

"Agnes Ann writes to them, too. Max and Woody, I mean. Because I asked her to. They've become great friends."

Rachel mashed her potato salad until it was flat but made no reply. Paul had been writing personal letters to Agnes Ann, but not to her. But then, she had been doing an awful lot of things with Simon, too, so maybe all those things evened out somehow. Maybe.

"Then there was me having to hide all the time because the place we rented didn't allow kids," Paul continued. "I spent hours and hours at the library because there wasn't any other place to go. That might sound like fun, especially when you like to read like I do ... I read all Simon's father's books. But day after day, with nothing much to eat ..." He filled his plate again before he went on.

"And Pop's drinking kept getting worse and worse, and he'd ... he'd hit my mother." He hung his head down, and Rachel saw a tear trace its way down his cheek. She started to go over and hug him again but decided it was better just to listen to him, the same way she'd listened to Simon Singer. Simon's words, "You've lived in the very same house, in the very same town, with the very same mother," kept ringing in her ears.

"Agnes Ann wrote me all about everything everybody was doing," Paul went on, "everything Odious Oxley said or did. She told me all about you and John Alan and Simon. How she never saw one of you without the other two ... what good friends you were." He looked up and smiled. "I was really glad you had them to take my place, Rachel. I really was."

"I know you were, Paul. I know you were. But how come you never told us?" Rachel asked as she began drawing circles with her fork around the edge of her still-full plate. "About Agnes Ann writing to you, I mean," she added without looking up.

"She asked me not to. I never was sure why. She said I was the first friend she'd ever had. And she thanked me, Rachel. All the time, she thanked me for being her friend. Thanked me for being her 'pen pal.' That's what she called me, her 'pen pal.' I know that sounds kind of silly, kind of sissy maybe even. But I sure looked forward to those letters of hers."

"Well, now I understand about Agnes Ann. Some of it, anyway. Mr. Schwartz says we all have secrets. But what about her daddy? Why did *he* go to all that trouble, Paul? Driving all the way to Amarillo in this awful heat? Giving you tires for free and putting them on?"

"He did it for Agnes Ann. Said she asked him to come help us, so he did. Her father loves her an awful lot, Rachel. I know that's hard for you to imagine, but it's the truth."

Paul pushed back from the table, stood up, and hooked his thumbs in the straps of imaginary overalls as he drawled, "Any friend of my girl Agnes Ann is a friend of mine." Rocking back and forth on his feet, he pretended to spit tobacco juice on the floor, and added, "Yes, sireee, my sweet little Agnes Ann is the apple of my eye."

Paul reached over and grabbed an apple from the fruit bowl in the middle of the table. He took a big bite and wiped the juice off his face with the back of his hand. Even his hands looked bigger than Rachel remembered.

"Remember, Rach, Grandpa Griggs used to call you that, too. The 'apple of his eye.'" He looked out the window instead of at her. "Sure wish he was still alive to come home to. But then we'd have to tell him about Pop taking off. Pop's the one who broke Granddad's heart, you know."

"Did ... did Mr. Billingsly drive you all home?" Rachel asked, trying to digest all she'd just heard.

"Nope. He did follow us, though. To be sure we made it. Mom drove."

"Your mother's learned how to drive a car? Your fraidy cat mama?"

"She learned all kinds of things in California, Rachel. You won't recognize her. She bleached her hair! She's a blonde now! Says blondes have more fun!"

"Your mother's a blonde? I don't believe it!"

"Being able to earn all that money ... even if Pop did gamble most of it away ... that's what changed her. Says she's going to get a job at Fort Sill, make something of herself. I keep telling her she's always been something to me, but she says this 'something' is different. I'm not sure what she means by that, but she sure seems to know."

"Simon said the Billingslys had good in them, and you're going to learn right away that everybody has to believe and do what Simon Green says." She grinned and reached over to touch his hair even though there wasn't much hair to touch. "If you don't do what Simon says," she added ominously, "they kick you out of the army and make you grow your hair out again."

"The army?" Paul laughed.

"It's a long story. We've got nine whole months worth of long stories to trade, and I got about a hundred 'cross your heart and hope to die' secrets to tell you."

"Cross you heart and hope to die?" Paul repeated

with a smile. "That's one I hadn't thought of since I left Oklahoma. We did that a lot when we were little, didn't we? Funny how you forget stuff like that."

There was another period of awkward silence before Rachel spoke again. "Well, I guess I'm going to have to figure out how to like your pen pal, Agnes Ann, too. Simon says I should, and as I said—what Simon says, we all have to do. It's not going to be easy, but I guess anything's possible. That's what Mr. Schwartz believes anyway. Anything is possible." She tried to keep the smirk off her face as she added, "It might even be possible those tires her father got you were not straight off the black market! It *might* be possible, but I doubt it!"

CHAPTER 27
Letter from the Past

November 4, 1943

Simon took the front steps to his house two at a time and didn't give a thought as to how many steps there were. Counting the steps, knowing his exact age in days, months, and years, even playing the parts of people who'd suffered great pain, were no longer necessary when his father returned from the war and his family was together again. Thanksgiving was only weeks away, and he had much to be thankful for.

His father, who had been injured on the third Friday the thirteenth of 1942 in the fierce Battle of Guadalcanal in the Solomon Islands, had been given a Purple Heart along with a medical discharge. Although Isadore Green had never lived in Apache, the town had thrown a grand party when he arrived and claimed him as a native son.

Since Simon was so happy in school, the Greens decided to stay in Apache, and his mother now played her violin day and night while his father worked on a new book. Simon had even been able to talk them into sending for Zinziberi, and she was to arrive by train in time to eat turkey with the rest of the family. And this very morning Agnes Ann had told him she thought his crew cut made him the handsomest boy in the seventh grade, and Paul had picked him to be on his team even if he was still the slowest runner in the class. In spite of the war, Simon Green's life was beautiful again!

He threw the front door open and bounded inside.

"Letter for you, Simon," his father announced even before the front door had time to snap shut behind him. Isadore Green held the small lavender-colored envelope in both hands as if it were too heavy for just one hand to hold. Simon's mother was seated on the couch. Her hands pressed a handkerchief to her mouth, and her eyes were red and puffy. Simon ignored the letter and went over to sit by his mother. His father followed him and sat down in the vacant spot on the other side. He placed the letter on his own knees, but they were bouncing up and down so badly it quickly fell to the floor.

Simon bent to pick it up. When he saw the German postmark and the name "Effie Weiss" printed in the upper left-hand corner with no return address, his heart began to pound so hard he thought his chest might burst. He flipped the envelope over and stared at the blank back for a full minute, a minute spent trying to draw air into his lungs before he had to turn the envelope over again. His father and mother seemed to have stopped breathing. There was no sound from either of them.

The name on the envelope, like the name on the postcard from the hungry people, was "Simon Singer." An "in care of" and his father's famous name had once again routed Simon Singer's mail through Isadore Green's publishing company. The postmark containing the date and place, stamped in German, were illegible.

"It came in that," his father told him, pointing toward a brown legal-sized envelope on the end table next to him, "addressed to me. So I opened it. There was a note from one of the mail sorters who had noticed the Simon Singer name, noticed ..." He shifted his gaze from Simon's face to his own feet as he pulled the postcard from the hungry people from under the brown envelope. "After this postcard came," he continued, still not looking up from his shoes as he handed the postcard to Simon, "I panicked at the thought that Simon Singer's family might escape and come to get him back. And yet, I wanted to help them. To send them 'something of bread.' But there was no way. No return address. I've never felt so helpless.

"When I left for the navy, I told my editor to have all my mail held in New York. I used the excuse of the war and crowded mailbags. But the truth was ... the truth is ... I was afraid another card would come. And you and your mother would get it. I ... I was afraid the next letter or card might have a return address, and I wouldn't be here to help you figure out what to do!"

He stopped and looked back into Simon's face again, into his eyes. "I am a very selfish man, Simon. Very selfish. But I loved you and your mother so much ... I love you so very much."

"I have seen the postcard," Simon admitted, picking up his mother's hand and giving it a squeeze. "I saw it over a year ago."

"Oh, Simon," Sylvia murmured.

He looked back and forth between his father and his mother.

"There was nothing I could do, no way I could send anything to people in a country Hitler had smothered. Bernard Singer had to know that." Simon's voice came out cold and hard.

There was a long period of silence.

"Effie's letter is addressed to Simon Singer," his father pointed out, as if Simon could not see that fact for himself. "So ... so we waited for him ... for you ... to get home." He bowed his head and put his hands on his still bouncing legs. "It's the hardest thing I've ever done in my life, waiting for you to open it," he whispered. "I wanted to know ... to know first ... but your mother ... Sylvie would not let me ..." His voice trailed off.

Simon stared at the letter. Until he opened it and read the truth, they were still alive. All of them. Still alive. And hungry. His father, his mother, his grand-mother, and Hannah. He'd always thought the final story, the truth, if the truth could ever be known, would come from Effie—Effie, who had shared so many stories with him and with Hannah. Now Effie was about to tell him one more story. He reached over and got his mother's hand and then his father's and put them on his upper arms to help steady him as he slowly opened the envelope.

"I think," he said softly, "I think, if you don't

mind, I would like to read it aloud. I'd like to imagine it was written to someone else, a boy I once knew long ago. A boy named Simon Singer."

They both squeezed his arms at the same time, and when they did, Simon Green squealed, but he did so very softly.

"I'm real," he whispered before he began.

"'September 14, 1943 ...'"

He paused to think a moment. "Less than two months ago," he said softly, before he continued.

"'Dear Simon, it has been such a long time since my sweet Peter Rabbit hopped out of my life, yet your forlorn little smile as we said *auf Wiedersehen* for the last time floats through my dreams still. I, of course, still picture you as a marvelously bright six-year-old rather than the young man who is approaching his teenage years, which you now must be.

"'Where to begin? I am sure your heart rose to your throat when you saw my name on this envelope. As wise beyond your years as you were, and must be even more so by now, you had to immediately suspect I would have news of your family. And you suspect, too (Oh, how I pray you are not reading this alone, that you are at this moment surrounded by people who love you, whom you love!) you suspect that the news is not good.'"

Simon stopped reading and imagined himself

242

crumpling the paper, crushing it into a ball, and throwing it into the crackling fireplace across the room. But he knew he could not do that. He had to be true to himself, even though he was not at all certain who that self was.

The father and the mother (why was he suddenly thinking of them like that?) had not moved, had not taken their hands away from his arms, but he could not bear to look at either of them. Not until he finished Effie's letter.

"'There is no soft or easy way to say this, my sweet Simon! I only wish I were there to tell you in person that ... that ...'" He stopped and handed the letter to his father to continue the sentence while Simon nestled in his mother's arms and wept hot and bitter tears.

"'... that your mother, your father, and your grandmother are all gone from this plane of existence,'" his father's voice went on, "'gone to a world where the birds sing day and night (you must remember how your mother loved birds!) and there is no war, no pain, no sorrow.'" His father stopped to wipe away his own tears, and Simon's mother began to rock him back and forth and croon softly to him as if he were a tiny baby.

"'While this chaotic war had produced many

false reports, of their deaths I am certain, Simon. Last month Hans had a long visit with one of the few survivors of the Ghetto Uprising in Warsaw and a good friend of your father's. By now, you must have read and heard about that place of eternal sorrow, a well too deep for tears and yet the tears keep flowing. According to an eyewitness, your father was among the last to die, one of the last to show the Nazis the amazing strength and incredible courage of those who love and value freedom more than life.

"'Your dear mother and grandmother were spared the agony of those last days. They both died early in the spring of the typhus which ravaged the Ghetto from its first days as a prison. The remains of all three of your dear loved ones rest inside that Ghetto in Warsaw, a ghetto which, with every story that escapes its walls, becomes more and more a monument to Jewish courage and bravery.'" Again, Isadore Green stopped to wipe his eyes.

"'While I am relieved to report that Hannah did not accompany them to Warsaw ...'"

Simon sat up quickly.

"'... that she was with Hans and me until seven months ago ...'"

"April!" Simon cried. "Hannah was alive this April! She saw the spring! She heard the robins sing!"

Isadore continued reading. "'But I do not wish to give you false hopes for her survival, as I have had no word from her since she left our house.'"

Simon crumpled into his mother's arms again.

"'As her twentieth birthday approached (I am sure it is hard for you to imagine her a grown woman, Simon, but she is that, grown and quite beautiful!) her restlessness grew. She knew Hitler had put his terrible curse on those who were crippled as well as those who were Jews, yet she chose to try to escape to freedom rather than live what little of her life she felt was left in hiding. She was your father's daughter in that, just as you are ...'" Isadore stumbled on the next words, but was finally able to finish, "'your father's son.'"

Isadore had to look to the ceiling and take several very long breaths before he could continue.

"'A young man named Peter (your grandfather and your favorite rabbit!) was involved in her decision to leave. She felt that even his name was a sign that she should go with him.'"

Isadore stopped reading to put his hand on Simon's head.

"A sign, Simon," he whispered, "a good sign!" He picked up where he left off.

"'This Peter is a strong and handsome boy. Hans

befriended him in the resistance and brought him home for a meal. He fell very much in love with your dear sister the first time they met. War forges strong and resilient love, sweet Simon. War causes the human spirit to realize how brief are our hours on this earthly journey so we love more quickly and strongly than ever we could love in peace. I storm the gates of heaven nightly that Peter was able to somehow smuggle our Hannah to safety, to the arms of those who could shield and protect her.

"'Now that I have had to unwillingly break your heart, dear Simon, let me close by saying that should I hear anything, anything at all from or about your dear sister, I will write to this same address again. I wish it were possible for you to write me and let me know you received this letter, but once we had to leave our home, Hans and I are never in the same place more than one night. We, too, are Jews, you know, walking the circus high-wire without benefit of net. Do you remember your dear father used to say that often?

"'I can only imagine the feelings you must have had for your father over the years, Simon, because of what he did in giving you away. You were so very angry and confused the last time I saw you, a broken-hearted little actor who tried to be brave for Hannah, tried to act as if you believed her when she said she would see you again.

"'Your father's decision, while it had to be made very quickly, was not done without a great deal of thought and agony. He met Max Burger the day he escaped from the concentration camp. A series of events rapidly unfolded in a way that made your father, who as far as I knew, had no belief in either a Higher Power or Divine Intervention, decide that both were possibilities and were suddenly shaping your life. He was desperate to find a place to send you, a place where you would no longer be a Jew and yet would know of your heritage, a place that would nourish the prodigy you had already shown yourself to be. Max Burger knew of such a place.

"'There are gaps in my story, sweet Simon. The years and our many moves have jumbled my memory. But I hope I have told you enough that you will be able to piece together your story like a patchwork quilt. That, in the end, is what all of our lives have become ... a piece of red velvet from our bedspread stage curtain, a brown scrap of burlap from your Billy Goats Gruff costume, a square from your mother's green wool skirt, all stitched together with the thread from your dear grandmother's sewing basket.

"'My hand is tired and the light grows dim. I

247

close with the prayer that you receive this story, perhaps the last story I shall ever be able to tell you, my sweet Simon.

"'All my love to my dear little actor—Effie.'"

Isadore folded up the letter very carefully, making sure the creases were just as they had been when it was opened.

"I didn't want to give you up, but God knows I did hope—believe me, Simon, I did wish that we could have saved them, too. All of them. Is it ... is it possible for you to forgive my selfishness?"

"I was going to leave you," Simon whispered.

"What did you say, Simon?" Sylvia asked, taking the handkerchief from her mouth at last and scooting forward on the sofa. "I couldn't understand what you said."

"I just remembered," he said, looking down at his hands. "That was my plan." He clutched his fists, thumbs up. "I planned to go back to Germany, to return to being Simon Singer."

They both stared at him, but neither of them said anything.

"The day you asked me to become your son, the day you told me the Nazis might come to America looking for me," he said, turning to face Isadore. "I had only been in your home two days, and you were asking me to give up everything I had ever known and loved."

Simon's father hung his head and allowed what tears he had left to flow silently down his cheeks. His mother's eyes were dry, but they never left his face.

"So, I decided to do as you asked. But I would just be *acting* the part of Simon Green, *pretending* to be the son you had always wanted." He got up and walked over to the window to look out at the leaves that seemed to be chasing each other across the winter lawn. "Then, when the opportunity came, I would thank you very kindly and go back to being Simon Singer again, go back to my *real* family." He unclenched his fists and rubbed his hands up and down the sides of his legs.

"I even called you *the* father and *the* mother in my head. I did that so I wouldn't mix you up with *my* mother and *my* father. We all became actors in a play." He stopped to look from one to the other, but they were both staring at the floor in front of them. "But then ... but then ... in no time at all you became real, my real father, my real mother. And I became your real son."

He picked up the lavender envelope which contained Effie's letter and pressed it tightly between his hands as if he were saying a prayer. "I will never forget them, though," he whispered in a voice that somehow sounded much younger than his own. "My mother, my father, my grandmother, my Hannah. No part of me will ever forget them."

CHAPTER 28
Anything Is Possible

November 1945

Simon heard a knock—a knock so soft he thought for a moment it might be the wind slapping one of the bare branches from the dying elm tree against the front door of the house, although he knew the tree was much too far from the house for that to be possible.

"Anything is possible," Mr. Schwartz's voice whispered to him once more as he put his book down, pulled himself out of the chair, and made his way to the front door. The dusky, late November sunlight filtered through the living room curtains, casting spider web shadows on the worn gray rug.

"Anything is possible." The last words Mr.

Schwartz had whispered to him just before he slipped into the "big sleep," as Kenneth's Kiowa grandmother called death. That had been almost two years ago, but Simon's memories of the old man were as bright and vivid as the gold Roman numerals on the grandfather clock he passed on the way to answer the door.

"Clocks really aren't of much value," he remembered telling the mother not long after he'd turned into Simon Green. Clocks signaled only the present. They knew nothing of the future.

"You are our family's future," his mother had told him the day he had been put on the boat to America eight years ago. Eight years. More happy than sad. More good than bad. More laughter than tears.

He opened the door cautiously, the years of fearing the Nazis still buried deep within his brain. He gave the strange young woman on the porch and the handsome young man beside her a polite, questioning smile before he noticed the doll she was cradling in her arm, before she took the first halting step toward him. He studied her face, the face of a pretty stranger. Until she smiled. She put her fingers to her lips and blew him a kiss with her right hand as she held his Solomon doll out to him with her left.

"Hannah!" he shouted as he swept his sister into arms that had never forgotten.

AUTHOR'S NOTE

Between 1934 and 1945 thousands of children were res-
cued from the crushing boots of Hitler's Nazis through both
individual and group efforts in various parts of Europe as
well as the United States. Britain arranged for 10,000 mostly
Jewish children, known as Kindertransports, to be brought
from their war-torn countries to England, where they were
placed with Jewish and non-Jewish families and in group
homes until the end of the war. Their story is told in the
Academy Award-winning documentary *Into the Arms of
Strangers.*

In America, due to prevailing anti-Semitic attitudes and
the depression, the efforts to save Jewish children were
made in a much smaller and more clandestine manner. For
example, Gilbert Kraus, a Philadelphia lawyer, orchestrated
the rescue of fifty Austrian children who were brought to
Pennsylvania under the sponsorship of the Brith Sholom
Lodge, a Jewish fraternal organization. These twenty-five
boys and twenty-five girls, all of whom arrived during the
summer of 1939, were Americanized and nurtured until they
could be reunited with family members.

In a much larger effort, more than 1,200 Jewish children were slipped onto ocean liners in groups of three to five

and brought into the United States. They came under the sponsorship of a variety of Jewish relief organizations which arranged for their placement in Jewish homes in order to preserve not only their lives but also their religious heritage.

The heart-rending plea written on the postcard Simon Green found came directly from a *real* postcard in my family's possession. In the tiny message box of that postcard, sent from Berlin to America shortly before Hitler's rise to power, my grandfather's brother wrote: "We are hungry. Please to send us something of bread." By the time he received this poignant card, my grandfather, Peter M. Levite, was unable to send "something of bread" because there was no place left to mail it. For over fifty years the postcard, along with the family's guilt about not being able to respond, was carefully preserved in a fireproof box inside a safe of Levite's Handy Corner general store in Apache, Oklahoma.

The story of the postcard's circuitous journey to Apache is a grand example of Divine Intervention. Wolf Levite of Berlin, the sender of the postcard, had two brothers in America: Peter M. Levite of Apache, Oklahoma, and Bernard Levite of Wichita, Kansas. Confusing the hometowns of his two brothers, Wolf addressed the postcard to Peter M. Levite in Apache, *Kansas*. Inexplicably, someone using a red pen marked through "Kansas" and wrote "Oklahoma" in big, bold letters, and the postcard made its way to the mailbox of my grandfather in Apache, Oklahoma.

While Simon Singer of *Simon Says* is a child born purely of my imagination, his story is one that so many actually lived. I hope the research I did in creating him allowed me to accurately portray the feelings and dreams of brave children of all ethnic backgrounds and religions who have been cut from their families' hearts by war.

TAPS

The characters in this books are fictional, but the town they live in, Apache, Oklahoma, is real. The real young men whose stars were turned from blue to gold should be remembered.

Winfard B. Anderson

Ralph L. Burkhead

Chester B. Holcomb

Gyle Wayne Kizer

Harry W. Mithlo

Wendell D. Moran

Melvin Myers

Ned Ivan Shafer

Joseph B. Stone

My sincere thanks to Rob Crews of Crews Funeral Home, who searched obituaries, Fairview Cemetery records, and Veterans' Administration headstones to find the names of Apache's heroes.

ACKNOWLEDGMENTS AND COMMENTARY

In writing historical fiction I'm called upon to weave actual dates, times, events, and places into the lives of people and animals who never actually existed, a delicate balancing act I find both enjoyable and frustrating. Since neither I nor any of the people I have created are in the least bit computer literate, I find myself telephoning experts in the field on a regular basis.

How else would I determine if a medium-sized dog urinating on a salt lick block would dissolve the block if the kind lady answering the phone at Ellison Feed and Seed had not listened to my question, staved herself from laughing hysterically, and seriously and conscientiously answered my question? Both Spot (whose innocence seems a bit suspect since he did pick a *yellow* block) and I were very grateful.

How could I ever figure out what Indian tribe the name Stumbling Bear belonged to (my father had a friend by that wonderfully descriptive name) if Kelly Farrell of the Apache library had not been kind enough to search it out for me? And when she informed me it was Kiowa, I certainly could not have done without the help of a linguist in that language, University of Oklahoma professor Gus Parker and his sparkly-eyed wife, Carolyn. Eleanor Barnes not only meticulously checked my German but also gave me great encouragement and feedback.

Poor Mr. Schwartz would have had little to eat or say had not Hymie Samuelson advised me on both Jewish dishes and Yiddish words. And my dear friend of days gone by, Harriet Reiter, did everything but tie the knots in Solomon's prayer shawl as well as furnish me phone numbers and addresses of people who helped me shape and mold Simon Singer/Green into the boy(s) he became.

I would need a whole chapter, a whole book perhaps, to thank the most valuable of Harriet's finds, Trude Turkel, whom I have come to know and love over a short period of time. Trude, who was sent to America by her parents in 1938 (she arrived two days before *Kristallnact*), opened her heart and mind to my every question and was willing to share her experiences and those of her younger brother, one of the Kindertransports sent to England.

Carol Burr, editor of *Sooner Magazine* at the University of Oklahoma, launched Simon on his journey by bringing me a newspaper clipping about OneThousandChildren.Org,™ which led me to Iris Posner, who gave of her time to read my manuscript and advise me.

As for the rest of my cadre, I can only say, as did the policeman in *Casablanca*, "Round up the usual suspects!"— the friends whom I have acknowledged in other books: Ann DeFrange, proofreader without peer; David Todd, who knows all the answers; Debby Wear, Linda Horton, and Sandra Sites, my Park on Main cohorts with Internet access;

and, as always, the amazingly patient staff at the information desk at Norman Public Library, to whom I present the toughest questions ever and who never ever fail me! Also, I am so grateful to Inez McCollum, who shared stories about my grandfather. Thanks for "the memories."

Virginia and Melissa, I saved you until the last because that's where the best belong.

GLOSSARY

American Legion Hall—building where military veterans and others hold meetings.

annihilate—destroy completely.

anti-Semitic—prejudiced against Jews.

aulgulmagaun—Kiowa for red-haired female.

Aryan race—In Nazi ideology, a member of a Caucasian Gentile race, especially of a Nordic type.

auf Wiedersehen—German for good-bye.

Beelzebub—the Devil.

beeswax—slang for a person's private business. Most often used in the phrase "None of your beeswax!"

belligerent—eager to fight.

blitz—German for lightning; in wartime, air-raid conducted with great intensity and ferocity; used specifically for the series of raids made by the German Luftwaffe on England in the early 1940s.

Brown-shirt—a member of the *Sturmabteilung*, a Nazi German militia founded in 1921, reorganized in 1930, and notorious for its violent methods. So called because of the brown shirt worn as part of the uniform.

by heart—memorized.

censor—to remove information that may be secretive or may pose a security risk.

Challah bread—yeast-leavened white egg bread usually braided, which is traditionally eaten by Jews on the Sabbath or holidays.

chew the fat—discuss something in detail.

circumstantial evidence—a series of events of circumstances which may indicate somone is guilty of a crime.

culprit—one who is charged with an offense or crime.

Cunningham, Glenn—Nicknamed "Kansas Ironman," Cunningham was one of the world's top middle-distance runners during the 1930s and won the prestigious Sullivan Award in 1933 as the nation's top athlete.

enigma—one who is puzzling or difficult to explain.

Evans, Dale—singing cowgirl movie star and wife of Roy Rogers.

Flag Day—In August of 1949, President Harry Truman issued a proclamation making June 14 Flag Day, a national holiday. Until then, individual states had observed that date, with Pennsylvania being the first state to adopt Flag Day in 1893.

flak—antiaircraft artillery.

Forty-fifth Division patch—changed in April of 1939 from the swastika to the Thunderbird.

gefilte fish—finely chopped fish mixed with crumbs, eggs, and seasonings.

Geneva Convention—The first Geneva Convention was held in 1864 with representatives of the major European powers in attendance. It established the neutrality of ambulances, hospitals, chaplains, and others engaged in care of the sick and wounded during warfare. All persons employed in such service are required to wear a Geneva cross—red cross on a white background—as a sign of their office.

Gestapo—Nazi internal security police, infamous for terrorist methods in dealing with anyone they felt was a threat to Hitler's Third Reich.

Gesundheit—German for health.

Guadalcanal—South Pacific island where one of World War II's fiercest battles was fought. It lasted for over six months. After it ended, the United States Navy never lost another battle to the Japanese.

Heil—German for welfare, safety, salvation.

Hoover, J. Edgar—FBI director from 1924 to 1972.

Houdini, Harry—magician and escape artist of the 1920s.

jargon—slang.

jitterbug—dance; also a word used as a political taunt against those apprehensive of war.

kosher—conforming to or prepared in accordance with Jewish dietary laws.

Kristallnact—night of broken glass, November 9, 1938, when Hitler telegraphed to the world he intended to exterminate all people he deemed unworthy of being part of his Master Race.

Lone Scouts—a branch of Boy Scouts of America for boys who live in isolated areas and therefore cannot be part of a regular Scout troop.

meshuga—Yiddish for crazy.

monologue—a play or part of a play in which only one person speaks on stage.

nau:com—Kiowa for good friend.

Nuremberg Laws—laws which stripped Jewish people of their citizenship and made them subjects of the Third Reich.

odious—deserving of hatred; abhorred.

Pandora's box—the mythical box that, when it was opened out of curiosity, released all that is evil into the world.

papoose—Native American infant.

Parker, Bonnie—girlfriend and partner of Clyde Barrow, famous bank robber of the early 1930s.

prejudiced—having a judgment or opinion that is not based on facts but on unreasonable beliefs.

Public Enemy Number One—top person on the FBI list of most wanted criminals.

qahiaulkaui Hitleroba—Kiowa name for Adolph Hitler; translates to "crazy madman."

radical—one who goes to the extreme limits to cause change.

Reich—German for kingdom, empire, realm.

salt lick—a block of salt set out in fields or barns for cattle, sheep, or deer to lick.

salvo—a simultaneous discharge of firearms; also a forceful oral or written assault.

Savo Island—The water around this island was renamed Ironbottom Sound because it was strewn with the remains of so many sunken vessels.

schwarz—German for black; with a capital letter, it means a black person.

Seder—the feast commemorating the exodus of Jews from Egypt, celebrated on first night of Passover.

S. S.—*Schultastaffel*; elite German military guards.

stateside—on or in the United States of America.

swabbies—slang for sailors.

swastika—a cross with a right-angled projection at the end of each arm, used as the symbol of Nazism. The word, which comes from Sanskrit "swastika," a derivative of svasti "well-being, luck," originally denoted an ancient cosmic or religious symbol of this form. English adopted it as the equivalent of German *Hakenkreuz,* literally "hook-cross." In 1932 thousands flocked to Hiter's *Hakenkreuz* (swastika), the anti-Semitic cross in a color scheme of red-white-black in memory of the colors of the old army.

Taci—Kiowa for maternal grandmother; paternal grandmother is *Talyi*; *Kogi* is the word for both maternal and paternal grandfather.

V-mail—Letters written by soldiers in World War II. These were scripted on special sheets of paper with glue along the sides so the single sheet formed both the letter and the envelope. The sheets were then photographed and transferred to microfilm for shipping, reducing the amount of space needed and therefore speeding up delivery time.

walkie-talkie—small, two-way radio transmitter which can be carried from place to place, allowing two people to talk with each other while walking.

War Time—On February 2, 1942, all the clocks in the United States were advanced one hour to save energy. This was a year-round form of Daylight Savings Time. It did not end until September 30, 1945.

ABOUT THE AUTHOR

Born in Apache, Oklahoma, the setting for four of her seven award-winning books, **Molly Levite Griffis** spent the winters of her childhood listening to stories told around the potbellied stove in Levite's Handy Corner, her parents' general store. Sweetened by jellybeans from the store's rolled glass candy case, Mrs. Griffis' summers were whiled away on the banks of Cache Creek, where she fished for crawdads with her daddy's handkerchiefs and honed her skills as a storyteller by inventing excuses for the fishy smell in the family's laundry hamper. Her older sister, Georgann, who didn't fish for crawdads with their father's handkerchiefs or ever do anything else naughty, was (and continues to be) her inspiration if not her role model.

A lifetime member of the Southwest Mustang Breeders Association, Mrs. Griffis has had many interesting careers. She taught English and history at all levels from fourth grade through college, established a publishing company which produced eighteen Oklahoma books in nine years, ran an independent bookstore whose bestsellers were Pendleton Indian blankets, and taught yoga as well as baton twirling until she decided a keyboard was easier on her fingers as well as her neck.

Mrs. Griffis is a graduate of the University of Oklahoma and lives in Norman, Oklahoma. She has two grown children, a red-haired daughter, who was the inspiration for Rachel, and a writer son who lives in the Czech Republic.